Goodbye Miami
Tales Of
An American Climate Refugee

I0665080

TREESONG

Cranncheol Publishing

ISBN-13: 978-0-692-19133-0

Cover art for Goodbye Miami by:
SelfPubBookCovers.com/RLSather

DEDICATION

This book is dedicated
to everyone who has taken action
in response to anthropogenic global warming
and to the present and future generations
of human and non-human life
who will inherit the world
created by our choices.

PREFACE

I remember the moment when the basic idea behind Goodbye Miami first came to me. I had already started working on my second novel, so I wasn't really looking for another big project. However, I often find myself daydreaming about various stories that I may or may not ever put down in writing. I also often find myself contemplating the ways in which my writing speaks to my values and the social and environmental justice issues of our times. One night, these thoughts were on my mind shortly after reading the Kindle compilation of a zombie fiction blog called Living With the Dead by friend and fellow author Joshua Guess. Suddenly, a thought occurred to me. What would a climate fiction blog look like?

As soon as I asked myself this question, my mind was flooded with answers. I've spent the better part of the past decade or so learning and talking about global warming. I co-host an environmental talk show called Your Community Spirit on a local community radio station called WDBX. Each week, I read the latest environmental news looking for interesting and important stories to talk about on the show. This usually includes a strong focus on stories about the climate crisis. I knew right away that I wanted the story to be set slightly in the future, in a time similar to our own but slightly further along in the downward spiral of climate disruption. The year 2030 occurred to me because of an article about the Solutions Project that referenced a goal of switching to 100% clean energy by 2030. I knew that I wanted to focus on the United States, both because I live here and because we are arguably the world's biggest contributor to the climate crisis. Miami was a natural choice because of its exceptional vulnerability to extreme storms and rising sea levels. As all of these ideas and details swirled around in my head, I felt a sudden excitement. I knew that I simply had to do this project, and I even knew what the title would be.

Goodbye Miami.

I reserved the domain name for the blog that night. After fleshing out some notes about major plot points I wanted to cover and other details I wanted to include, I created the site and made my first entry. The rest is history.

I wrote Goodbye Miami with several goals in mind. As always, my main goal was to tell an interesting story. I believe quite strongly in the power of fiction to explore life's great questions and pressing concerns. Fiction can be a wonderful tool for encouraging personal and social change. However, it must always strive to do so in the context of an engaging narrative. Many of the greatest authors I've ever read have combined an exceptional skill at storytelling with an exceptional commitment to exploring meaningful questions about the societies in which they live and the direction in which those societies are headed. Though I have yet to achieve their mastery of the craft, I do hope to continue in their time-honored tradition of combining good storytelling with meaningful social and philosophical commentary.

Another notable goal, of course, was to inspire thought, conversation, and action in response to the climate crisis. Global warming is already happening; human activity is the primary cause of this warming; and the consequences of this warming pose a catastrophic threat to the continued survival and flourishing of human and non-human life. While this book is a work of fiction, the crisis that inspired it is real. All of the problems and solutions explored in Goodbye Miami are inspired by real-world problems and solutions associated with the climate crisis. Whether you agree or disagree with any particular part of this story, I hope you will find it a fruitful source of reflection, discussion, and inspiration to action.

There is not a single person or organization on this entire planet that has all of the answers to the global climate crisis. Honestly, at this point in history, the prognosis looks grim. However, we are a very creative and resilient species. There are billions of us alive today, and we can all do our part to improve the situation. If enough of us take this problem seriously, believe that we have the power to make a difference, and get to work on projects of resilience and resistance, hopefully we can find the solutions together.

If you have any questions or comments about this story and the issues it explores, I invite you to contact me. I do my best to respond to every message I receive from my readers. I look forward to hearing from you.

With that said, I hope you enjoy Goodbye Miami!

ACKNOWLEDGMENTS

Thank you to my wife, Grace, for being so supportive of my writing, my quirky superhero adventures, and all other aspects of my life.

Thank you to my daughter, Bedelia, for re-invigorating my appreciation for life and my commitment to do more to respond to the climate crisis.

Thank you to my readers, whether you've been with me from the beginning or this is the first time you've read one of my books.

Thank you to my Patreon backers for your ongoing support. This project predates my Patreon campaign, but your support and feedback helps keep me inspired to write and to publish my writing.

Thank you to Joshua Guess for writing Living With the Dead, the compelling zombie fiction blog that inspired me to think about what a climate fiction blog would look like.

Thank you to all of the people who are making positive contributions to our response to the global climate crisis. Climate scientists, climate activists, climate policy wonks, climate news sites and commentators, climate artists, climate educators, climate game designers, clean energy advocates, ecological agriculture practitioners, forest defenders, tree planters, and beyond. Your wonderful work helps me understand what is happening, what we can do about it, and what I can contribute through my writing, advocacy, and action.

GOODBYE, MIAMI
June 10, 2030 at 11:23

Goodbye, Miami.

My name's Kass and I'm a survivor of Hurricane Florence. Needless to say, I just had the craziest weekend in my whole entire life.

On June 6, 2030, a Category 5 hurricane made landfall in southern Florida. Even with modern disaster protocols in place, it'll still take weeks to figure out just how many people were killed and how much property was destroyed. Early estimates suggest that at least 700 people died in the storm itself and many more died in the aftermath. Tens of thousands of others have been displaced by storm damage. A hundred times that number will ultimately be displaced permanently if state and federal officials can't find a way to deal with the flooding and power outages.

Unless Homeland Security has a fifty billion gallon Shop-Vac, there's nothing they can do.

The city of Miami is currently underwater. Of course, everyone on Fox News says that we're being alarmists. "It's only a few feet," they say. "It'll be cleaned up in no time," they say. "There are still some dry spots," they say.

But I've lived in Miami my whole life. I've also been reading about global warming since I was a little girl. Sea level keeps rising faster and faster. I've been saying for years now that this was going to happen. It was only a matter of time. There's no getting that water out of there permanently and no chance for a real recovery if most of the city is underwater.

And so, just like that, Miami has fallen, and I've become an American climate refugee.

They have a FEMA camp farther inland for the refugees with nowhere else to go. Luckily, though, I have a cousin in Illinois who's taking me in as her roommate. Illinois isn't really my cup of tea, but it beats going to a FEMA camp. And Alejandra es mi chica favorita, so there's that. I haven't seen her offline in years! I'm really looking forward to seeing her smiling face again. She's like the sister I never had.

Anyway, I'm getting really tired. It's been an exhausting weekend and this train is so much more comfortable than the bus was. I'll post more about my crazy weekend next time. In the meantime, all my thoughts and prayers go out to the other survivors and the only city I've ever called home.

Hurricane Florence, Day 1
June 10, 2030 at 23:15

I finally made it to Illinois, thank God. When I was a kid, it wasn't such an ordeal to get across the country. Domestic flights used to cost less than a month's pay. Passenger trains ran more often because more people could afford them. There was also a lot less of this ridiculous suspicion about people crossing state lines. We're all still one big happy American family, right? For now, anyway.

Also, did you know that Illinois is 395 miles long from north to south? I knew this intellectually, of course. I used to visit Alejandra a lot in Chicago. But now she lives in a college town that's closer to St. Louis than Chicago. As I stepped off the train this afternoon, I noticed a distinct lack of tall buildings. Also, not surprisingly, there's no sign of the ocean. Not yet, anyway.

I'll talk more about my new home and new life here once I've had the chance to get settled. In the meantime, I was going to tell you about my last days in Miami.

Last Thursday started out as a day like any other. Yes, there was a hurricane warning. But it's hurricane season. Even before we really started noticing the effects of global warming, a hurricane in June was nothing unusual. You watch the weather reports, stay indoors, maybe board up some windows if you own a house or storefront. Such is life in Miami.

But then all hell broke loose. Nobody expected Hurricane Florence to gain so much intensity so quickly. Even as the storm made landfall, local newscasters were reopening the age-old debate about whether it was time to create a Category 6 for hurricanes. And then, of course, they were presumably hiding under their desks and praying for their lives like the rest of us.

For anyone who cares about the numbers, the winds reached 176 m.p.h. and the storm surge reached 18 feet. But numbers can't convey the reality of what we experienced on the ground. Florence laid waste to Miami like something out of a movie. Even before Florence, we were having constant problems with flooding due to sea level rise, a fact which most people don't even bother denying anymore. But as soon as Florence hit, everything was underwater.

I was in my apartment when it happened. Our landlord didn't do much to prepare for the storm, so I got a front row seat to the action. The wind shattered my front window really quickly. Luckily, I had some foamboard taped to the window, so the glass didn't go flying everywhere. But once the window was blown out, I could hear the wind howling like a big hungry demon that was devouring the city I love. The rain soaked everything in the living room and I could hear terrible crashing and crunching sounds outside over the din of the storm.

I didn't see anything at first because I was hiding under my desk. I don't know how long I was sitting under that desk clutching my knees to my chest and saying more Hail Marys than I've said in the whole rest of my life. I'm not a very religious person, but it was one of those moments, you know?

When things finally settled down, I looked out my window to see a different city. Several feet of standing water had filled the streets with bits of broken buildings, overturned cars, trash, and who knows what else. Honest to God, I think I saw a dead body floating in the water down the block. Thankfully it passed out of sight before I could be sure. There was no power, no running water, no cellphone service, and no safe way to get out of the building because of the floodwaters.

My first response was shock. I must have spent a few minutes just staring out that window, mesmerized by the eerie silence punctuated by occasional shouting and crashing in the distance. Then, I remembered something.

I was prepared.

Living in Miami teaches you to prepare for storms. Living in Miami and spending your whole life learning about global warming teaches you to prepare for apocalyptic storms. Unlike most people I know, I had an entire closet filled with preparedness supplies. Highlights include:

- Several cases of MREs, these little meals in a bag that they originally designed for the military
- Emergency bottled water (10 gallons plus a gallon or two in my kitchen water cooler)
- Portable water purifier and water purification tablets
- First aid kit with extra supplies
- Multitool and small toolbox with other tools
- Rope, twine, and other small but useful supplies
- Laminated map of my neighborhood
- Hand-crank emergency radio and HAM radio
- Hand-crank LED flashlight
- Emergency flares
- Suitcase-sized portable solar charger
- Passport, birth certificate, and a few other documents in physical and digital form
- About half of my life savings, which unfortunately was not much.

- Self-inflating life raft

Even for me, an avid prepper, that last item seemed way over the top when I bought it. But it was on sale secondhand, so why not? I knew Miami would flood like this eventually. I just didn't know it would be this soon. Besides, even if it never happened, my long-term plans included spending retirement on a boat somewhere along the coast.

Thanks to Florence, I was living the dream ahead of schedule.

That's all I have time for tonight. Alejandra said she was going to bed soon which is why I started writing. But now she wants to talk some more about what happened and our plans for the rest of the week. Maybe talking to her will help me focus my thoughts as I get to the hard parts of this story. In the meantime, wish me luck in my new home here in small town southern Illinois. This is going to take some adjusting, but with Alejandra by my side, I can do anything.

HURRICANE FLORENCE, DAYS 1.5 AND 2
June 11, 2030 at 23:36

My first full day here with Alejandra in Illinois was great. We went shopping for a few essentials, saw a few sites, and went out for dinner together, her treat. She says she'll introduce me to the bar scene this weekend when there's more going on. In the meantime, we just went home and spent an hour or two setting up my new room in what used to be her home office. She's so sweet, moving her desk into her bedroom just so I could have a place to stay.

Anyway, back to the story of Hurricane Florence.

So there I was, staring out the window, when I remembered my prepper supplies. I ran to the closet, checked everything over, and considered my options.

I don't know my neighbors in my building very well, but I decided to start with them. Most of them weren't home because it was still early on a weeknight. But I did find four other people and share a few water bottles and small bandages for two of them.

Then I decided to check out the neighborhood.

Walking around in floodwater is a bad idea. You never know what might be in the water — raw sewage, jagged edges, needles, maybe even jellyfish washed in from the ocean. So as strange as this sounds to someone who's never been there, I decided to use my raft to explore the neighborhood. I'd never used a self-inflating raft before, so it was surreal to watch it puff up so quickly. In just a few minutes, I was paddling my way down the street looking for survivors.

It's funny how when disaster strikes, instinct kicks in. You learn more about who you really are. When I bought those supplies, I was buying them for myself. But once I knew I was fine, my first thought was to go out into the neighborhood and help people. My dad was a nurse and my mom was a community organizer, so maybe it's in my blood.

I took my big first aid kit, some water, and some MREs with me on the raft. I saw a few groups of people starting to walk around in the floodwaters and warned them of the dangers. Then I met this cute older couple who seemed like tourists. They had no idea where they were going and the woman had a badly skinned knee. With her partner's help, I carefully lifted the woman up into the raft with me and cleaned and bandaged her knee. The man wouldn't fit in the raft, so he walked alongside us as I paddled toward the nearest hospital.

That's how the first few hours after the storm went. I helped that couple to the hospital, helped a woman find her teenage boy who had been at a friend's house, and gave out all the food and water that I had left with me. As it was getting dark, I decided it wasn't safe to be outside anymore, so I headed back home.

The first night was surreal. I felt safe at first because I still had plenty of food and water. I also had fully charged phone and tablet thanks to my solar charger. If the phone or internet came back on, I'd be ready to talk to the outside world for as long as I wanted.

But then there were the screams. The screams bothered me the most. I heard a few crashing and breaking noises, like something falling over or maybe someone breaking into a building. No big deal. But every once in a while, I would hear someone in the distance yelling or screaming. I also heard gunfire — sometimes before the screams, sometimes after. And a few times, I heard motorboats nearby.

After a while, I boarded up the window as best as I could with foamboard and turned on the radio to hear the latest news. The announcer said that police, National Guard, and private contractors had been called in to maintain order. The water was high enough that you couldn't drive, but low enough that an ambitious person could walk or swim through the streets, which was a bad combination for law enforcement. I'd had a busy day, so eventually, I fell asleep listening to the radio.

I woke up the next day to the sound of neighbors having an argument. It was already mid-morning, which was strange because I'm usually an early bird. As I ate breakfast and listened to the radio, I decided that if the situation wasn't better by tomorrow, I'd leave town.

The afternoon and early evening of the second day were a lot like the first few hours of the first day. There were more people on the street, though, as people started looking for supplies, lost loved ones, and so on. I did some more patrolling on my raft and was pleased to see some police and paramedics on rafts and boats. I had heard about them on the radio, but this was the first time I saw them. As soon as they saw my raft, they asked me to help. I spent all day helping the paramedics transport injured people, medical personnel, and supplies from place to place. Then when it was dusk, they told me that there was a curfew and suggested I go home. At first, I kept volunteering because they were so short staffed and there was so much to do. But when it was fully dark out, I finally headed home.

I should have left sooner.

I was in sight of my apartment when I heard the buzz of the engine behind me. Suddenly, there was a floodlight pointed at me and a man speaking over a loud bullhorn.

"You are in violation of curfew. Put your hands up and step away from the vehicle."

I sighed, raising my hands over my head. It was at that point that I realized his request was impossible. How could I get out of the raft without using my hands?

I started telling him as much, but he interrupted. "I said get out of the boat! Habla ingles? Vete de tu bote!"

I climbed awkwardly out of the raft, stepping into the filthy floodwaters that I had mostly avoided for the past day and a half. The floodlight and bullhorn voice were coming from a small motorboat with several men on it. I assume they were men, although I could barely see them even when I shielded my eyes from the floodlight. They were dressed in black from head to toe.

The man in charge proceeded to grill me. Why was I out after curfew? Where did a [blank] like me get a raft like that? At first, I was relieved when he told me to leave. But then as soon as I put my hand back on my raft, he shouted at me to step away and go home.

The man intended to steal my raft.

In a lot of ways, I guess I've lived a sheltered life. Because for a minute there, I actually started arguing with him. I reached to grab my supplies out of the boat.

Then he fired his weapon.

Thank God it was only a warning shot. But it was a warning shot with some sort of automatic rifle. I'm not a gun person, I don't know what it was and couldn't see it clearly behind the floodlights. But I heard several loud explosions from his direction and heard impacts on the wall a few yards behind me. I ducked for cover, dunking my whole body in the water for a moment as I covered myself and started scrambling and half-swimming away. The men on the boat laughed. I put as much distance between myself and them as possible. When I finally looked back, I saw them pulling my raft out of the water and speeding away.

Okay, this is getting longer than I meant it to be. I'll have to leave off there for now. Time to get a late night snack, say goodnight to Alejandra if she's still up, and go to sleep.

Hurricane Florence, Day 3
June 12, 2030 at 07:23

Okay, where was I?

Those men had just stolen my raft from me. Once the shock wore off, I realized that they must have been working for Bastion – formerly known as Academi, Blackwater, and half a dozen other names. Ever since Hurricane Katrina, these mercenaries have been appearing on the streets of American cities in the wake of disasters. They're supposedly there to keep order, but they're just lawless bands of armed men doing whatever their bosses tell them to and whatever they can get away with.

I'm not trying to be political here. All I know is they stole my raft. That's enough for me.

I spent the rest of the night in my apartment listening to the news. Still no power, no cell towers, nothing. Emergency services were hopelessly overloaded and the National Guard and Red Cross still didn't have much of a presence on the ground. In other words, no real news, which was not good. So I read a book by hand-cranked flashlight and eventually went to sleep.

I woke up to the sound of my phone ringing. For a moment, I was still half-asleep and didn't realize how strange and important that sound was. Then I bolted upright and grabbed my phone.

It was Alejandra! She had been trying to reach me since the storm hit. She wanted to know if I was okay. She apologized for calling so early, but we were both so relieved that she had gotten through.

We talked for over an hour. While we were talking, I pulled the foamboard off of my window and looked outside. It was just after sunrise. The water was still almost as high as it had been immediately after the storm. There was still no sign of power.

I knew it was time to follow through with my plan.

So I went to my closet, grabbed my bugout bag, added as many extra supplies I could carry, and poured some water into the empty two gallon bottle from my kitchen. Then I grabbed my solar charger, tablet, and phone, put them in a bag, and headed out the door.

That was the start of the longest walk in my life. I walked for hours and hours to get out of Miami. I heard that the buses were still running in Ft. Lauderdale, so I knew I would have to walk there. Through a few feet of water. Carrying a lot of gear. Past all types of looters and Bastion and God knows what else.

Thank God I was in good shape. And thank God that there were some long stretches of road that were actually above water. There were hundreds of us heading north on foot, maybe a few thousand by the time night fell. I talked to a few of them, but the crowd was mostly quiet. It was a solemn procession. We all knew we had to get to Ft. Lauderdale and we all knew we had to do it before dark.

It had just gotten dark outside when I made it to the bus station. Chaos ensued as too many people tried to get on too few buses. People argued, people fought, people pleaded for a seat for their children. There were dozens of extra buses — some from companies, some from the government, some diesel, some electric. There was even a big red double decker bus there for some reason. I really wasn't sure where they all came from or what all of the options were. All I know is that I paid about two month's pay in cash for a single bus ticket from Ft. Lauderdale to New Orleans. Those who didn't have the cash got left behind and probably ended up in the FEMA camp.

So that's how I made it out of Miami. The bus took me to New Orleans and the train took me to southern Illinois. Alejandra met me at the station with a change of clothes and took me to her apartment on the edge of town. It's small apartment for two people, but it technically has two bedrooms, and she gave me the one that she was using as her home office. That was so sweet of her. She's three years younger than me, so I used to always be the "big sister" who was watching out for her. Now she's the one watching out for me. Thank you, Alejandra. If it weren't for you offering me a place to stay, I might still be stuck in Miami!

ANYTHING BUT MIAMI
June 13, 2030 at 20:30

Now that I've told you about my last days in Miami, I should tell you about my first days in Illinois.

My cousin, Alejandra, has been such a great host. She picked me up at the station, gave me new clothes, and gave me a place to stay. She has two jobs — one at a community center and one at a food co-op — so she's busy most of the day. But when she comes home at night, we talk, eat dinner, and usually go out somewhere too. It makes me feel very welcome in a place that's still unfamiliar to me.

Growing up, we used to be like sisters, except for the fact that I would only see her during summer vacation and sometimes for a few days around Christmas. When we were visiting, we would go to the movies together, watch TV together, read books together, play games together. We were inseparable. Now that we're in the same zip code again, it feels like old times.

The big difference is location. I've always been a city girl. I've spent my whole life living in Miami. Whenever I traveled, it was usually a big city. Alejandra and my aunt and uncle were all in Chicago. My one other aunt was in New York. I went to Europe and South America when I was in college and decided to max out my credit cards in search of adventure. I almost stayed in Buenos Aires, but that's another story for another day.

This is not a big city. It's a college town called Carbondale at the southern end of Illinois. It's farther south than St. Louis and sometimes it feels like I'm in the South. There are only about 30,000 people here and most of them are college students. Now that Alejandra has spent a few days showing me around, I'm starting to see what she likes about it. She fits in very well here and everyone seems friendly. But it seems so strange being in a place with no tall buildings, no real neighborhoods, no night life, not as much going on as you would have in a city. I don't even usually spend that much time going out, but somehow it feels strange not having any of that here. Especially the ocean! I already miss the ocean — the smell of it, the sight of it, the feel of it. How can people relax and clear their heads without going for a walk on the beach or just having a drink and looking out at the waves?

I think I know why I feel so homesick. I really shouldn't. Alejandra has been such a good host, and when I stop and think about it, there's a lot going on here for such a small town. But I feel homesick because for the past few days, whenever Alejandra's at work, I've been watching and reading all the news about Miami.

It's so heartbreaking. The number of dead keeps going up. They think it's more like 900 now. And the estimates of people displaced are going up too. The water went down somewhat after the storm, but now it's holding steady. There are a few feet of standing water throughout most of the city. So even though the storm didn't actually destroy most of the homes, it flooded them to the point where you can't realistically live in them. So those people will have to find new homes eventually. And there may be a few million of them.

Take me for example. The damage to my building wasn't too bad — a few broken windows, maybe some damage to the roof, mostly superficial. Fixable. But there's still three feet of standing water on our block! How do I get in and out without walking through nasty flood water? And how do they fix the power and internet? This is why I left.

And this is why so many are leaving. The first FEMA camp is full. Now there's another FEMA camp, and maybe another one after that. Some people are staying in Miami, but more are leaving. Even with all of FEMA's planning for disasters, it's hard to know what to do when something this big actually happens. It's chaos. Part of me wishes I were still there helping, but part of me is glad I didn't end up in a crowded shelter eating a meal a day and wondering what will happen next.

I need to stop spending so much time thinking about this, at least for a day or two. I've been reading and watching it all for hours and hours. It's not healthy. I thought that writing about it would help, and it did help, but now I need a break. When Alejandra gets home from work, I need to watch some mindless movies with her. Or go to the bars with her. Or go for a walk with her. Or talk with her about her day at work, or her love life, or anything at all, really.

Anything but Miami.

BETTER DAYS AHEAD
June 14, 2030 at 20:08

Today has been a much better day. I had a long talk with Alejandra last night over a few mojitos. She helped me realize that I'm more than just homesick. Ever since leaving Miami, I've been feeling survivor's guilt and a sense of helplessness. Talking about it and writing about it has helped. The next big step is getting active again.

I'm an active person. Back in Miami, I had three jobs: electric vehicle technician, my therapeutic massage practice, and some part time canvassing and odd jobs for a few green groups. That was quite a juggling act that kept me very busy. It usually added up to about 50 or 60 hours per week. I could have just stuck with two jobs and saved myself some time. But I like to stay busy and I like to have savings. So I just kept learning new skills that related to my interest and could earn me a decent living.

So what I need most is to get active again. I don't know long I'll stay in Illinois, so I don't want to make any serious commitments. But I could use at least a month here while I figure out my plans. Maybe I'll just stay for the summer and save up some money before moving to a new city or going back to what's left of Miami. I really do want to go back to Miami eventually, even if it's just to help with the recovery for a while. But it will take some preparation.

Alejandra has a few ideas about where I could work and volunteer here in southern Illinois. We can work on it over the weekend and next week. In the meantime, she says there are a lot more people and music at the bars on the weekends. I'll believe it when I see it. Either way, I'm sure we'll have a good time. We always do.

GOOD NEWS AND BAD NEWS
June 16, 2030 at 20:45

My first thought on Friday was that the weekend is not the best time to apply for jobs, especially in a small town like Carbondale. What I can do, though, is look around and ask around. So I decided to do just that.

So far, I've got good news and bad news.

The bad news is that the electric vehicle tech market and therapeutic massage markets are both saturated here. About ten years ago, the automotive school at the local university, SIU, switched its focus away from internal combustion to electric. It started with just one or two people teaching electric, but the spike in demand lead them to convert the whole department. Ever since then, they've graduated a lot of new techs each year. That wouldn't be a big deal in a big city, but there's not enough demand for them in southern Illinois. They have to go to St. Louis, Chicago, Memphis, and so on.

There are a lot fewer electric cars here in southern Illinois. I'd say maybe two thirds of the cars run on gas. It's strange seeing so many gas guzzlers zipping around, roaring and rumbling, making even the small streets of Carbondale smell like so much car exhaust. It reminds me of when I was a teenager and it was always like that. The national average nowadays is over half electric, with about two thirds of new vehicles being electric. But some people in southern Illinois resisted green tech early on because they were so into coal. They had generations of coal miners here, people who built their whole families on that way of life. And the coal and oil and gas companies kept telling them that it was the best way for them to get jobs and keep jobs in a dirt poor region. They made them all sorts of promises about clean coal, safe fracking, and so on.

But the fossil fuel companies lied, of course. They lied to everybody. And now there are a lot of rural areas like southern Illinois trying to catch up and clean up after the companies came and ruined their land and their communities. It's sad, really. I'm not political, but I do hope they finally put some of those people in jail. They keep talking about it, and they keep fighting in the courts and Congress to figure out what we should do with an industry that basically wrecked the entire world. But a lot of them are still too rich and powerful to catch. How do you catch the people who pay the politicians to get elected?

Anyway, I was talking about my job search. I don't know why the therapeutic massage market is saturated here. Maybe they teach it somewhere around here. I've seen some ads for other massage therapists and their prices are really low relative to what I'm used to in the city. I guess cost of living is lower here too. But still, it wouldn't be my first choice. I'm trying to save up money for a new start. Doing massage here would involve building a new client base, finding a good space to work out of, and so on. It would be more of a long-term project. I might call the one massage place just to see what they say about renting space, but I'll probably just stick with other options.

I'll go ahead and finish with the good news. I have at least two really good leads. Alejandra told me about one and I found the other one.

The first one is quick and easy: canvass and volunteer for local nonprofits. Alejandra works at a community center where a lot of nonprofits meet or have offices. She says that at least one of them is looking for part-time people to do canvassing in Carbondale and smaller towns in the area. I used to do that in Miami so that would be great.

The one that I found is more exciting: solar roadways! I was shopping at the food co-op when I met this guy named Ermete. He told me that the first municipal solar roadways are coming to Carbondale next month and that they'll need as many experienced workers as possible. I spent a summer doing solar roadways in New York, and that's more experience than most people around here have since it's new here. There are a couple of parking lots and driveways here, but nothing municipal yet. I'm really excited that I can be involved in bringing solar roadways to Carbondale! I just have to hope that this guy's right and then wait a month to get started.

That was a really long entry. I guess I had nothing better to do on a Sunday afternoon than write about all the things I learned over the past two days. Writing is about all I can do until the work week starts tomorrow. I'll let you know how it goes. In the meantime, if you're reading this, feel free to leave a comment. It would be good to know if anyone's listening.

GAIA HOUSE
June 18, 2030 at 14:30

The place where Alejandra works is called Gaia House. It's a community center for people of all beliefs. They have Christians, Jews, Muslims, Hindus, Buddhists, and more. They even have atheists and agnostics, although obviously those people don't have any worship services. They just have discussions.

The center also has a strong social justice and environmental focus.

Alejandra works there in a social work office. They do a lot of things out of that office to help people who are poor, homeless, jobless, and so on. Some of it's basic common sense help, like getting them a shower, some clothes, an ID if they don't have one. But some of it's a lot more complicated, like finding them a job, getting them treatment for drug addiction, and so on. I knew she worked in something like that, but it was good to get a peek at her office.

They also have all of these strange environmental projects! I thought I was well-educated about all that, but apparently not. They have a big yard, but it doesn't have any grass. It just has all of these gardens. Part of it looks like a lawn from far away, but when you get closer, you notice that it's a few different plants short plants, including clover. And you can eat it all! They also had some type of columns that plants grew on, raised vegetable gardens, mushrooms, bees, and more. There was even something called a food forest. It had trees and vines and bushes that all grew food. Some of the trees weren't fully grown yet, but a few had fruit, and I could see where they were going with it. It was like going to a science fair, but for green projects. And that's how it is every day over there.

They also had a big display listing their classes and workshops. Some were free and some were paid. I need to save up, so I'll probably pass on the paid ones. But maybe I'll go to the free ones. I have some time on my hands while I figure out my next step.

Anyway, to make a long story short, they said that they probably have part-time work for me! They actually only have a few paid staff, which is surprising given how much is going on there. But each project comes up with its own budget, and there's usually at least one project with a budget for part-time help. Right now the only thing like that is canvassing for a green group. It's not a lot of hours, but it's something. They'll call me to confirm it later in the week.

That's all that I have for today. I'll probably post something tomorrow about the latest news from Miami. I haven't been fixating on it lately, which is good. But I do read a little bit every day, and I want to talk about it tomorrow. I'll read some more tonight and post about it tomorrow after more job hunting.

THE NEW MIAMI
June 19, 2030 at 23:53

I had a good day today. The rest of my job hunting was completely unsuccessful , but that's not surprising given the state of the local economy. And the national economy, and the global economy. I enjoyed my day though because I got to explore the town. I still don't want to live here permanently, but it's a nice little spot to spend a couple of months with hanging out with mi prima and saving up a little cash. Even in the summer, there are plays, live music, outdoor concerts, all types of things to do. It's so hot and humid here though! I thought it would be more like Chicago. I guess it's 300 miles south, so why should it be like Chicago?

I said I'd talk about Miami today. I'm not sure what there is to say, but I'll try.

Miami is still underwater. When the storm surge receded, the water levels went down, and there are actually a few more spots above water than there used to be. But now it's holding steady at a few feet in most places. And it's not going to change anytime soon.

Sea level has risen much faster than they originally expected. I haven't done any academic research to confirm this, but just by reading the articles from the past few decades, it seems like the scientists kept being conservative at first and then revising their projections up, up, up. First it was 2°C by 2100 and maybe a foot of sea level rise. Then it was 3°C and maybe two feet. Now we're on track for 6°C by 2050 and maybe a foot each decade on top of the several feet we've already had. The world is changing, and anyone who denies it isn't taken seriously anymore.

I remember when I was in high school and they announced the start of the collapse of the West Antarctic ice sheet. That was one of the major turning points. Most of the adults didn't pay much attention at the time, but a lot of us who were in our teens and twenties were really thinking about how it might change our future. What will the world be like when I get out of college? When I get a job? When I buy a house? Will any of that ever happen if the economy keeps getting worse? Should I even have kids in such a world?

Anyway, back to Miami.

There's enough water on the ground that they can't reasonably expect to remove it in the foreseeable future. South Florida sits on a bunch of porous limestone. You can't keep the water out with a storm wall like they're doing in New York. It seeps in the ground and finds a way to bubble up everywhere. It has a mind of its own. The beaches have been mostly ruined by this for years. And now the beaches are just underwater, along with most of the city.

It's not an absurd, cartoonish, disaster movie type of flooding. You can still see all the buildings. Almost all of them are still standing. You can even walk around in most places if you don't mind walking in floodwater. But it's enough to shut down the city. You can't drive around in it. It gets in all the wells and pipes and electrical conduits and walls. It ruins everything.

Miami is starting to take on a new form. Most of the people who used to live there have become refugees. All of the cities further north like Orlando that didn't get flooded as much by the ocean are just flooded with refugees. Those who didn't have money for bus tickets or a place to stay have ended up in the camps. From the pictures and videos, Miami looks like a ghost town. It's the middle of the day and you don't see much happening at all downtown. It's very strange.

The boats are even stranger. Instead of cars now, they use boats to go everywhere. I guess it's not too strange since I grew up in Miami and I'm used to seeing boats all the time. But it's so strange to see them get out of the harbor and just go for a ride through the city. It's mostly just smaller motorboats, and mostly just police, National Guard, and Bastion. But still, it's strange to see.

One exciting thing that I saw was this long green boat called the Green Boatbus. It's run by a nonprofit and it's so slick and professional that they must have put it together before Florence. It's this long green boat that's about as long and wide as a large passenger bus. It has an electric motor, charging for phones and tablets, ample seating, wheelchair accessible, and a solar panel roof. It's almost as cheap as a bus too, but they're making big money by going all around the city and acting like a taxi for the people with more money. If you have money, you get to travel point to point like a taxi. If you're broke, you just have to wait a while to get to your destination. It's not ideal, but it's one of the few forms of travel left for people who don't own a boat and don't want to risk the waters.

There are a lot of problems and questions in Miami. I've heard about some of it from the news and some of it from friends who stayed behind. There are food shortages because people are running out of the food they had in their homes and grocery stores aren't open. Most of the police stayed, but they don't have enough boats. There aren't enough National Guard around because so much of the state has been affected in one way or another and so many are deployed overseas. Bastion is picking up the slack, but God help us if that's who's going to be in charge of Miami now. There are rumors of them shooting looters and taking the supplies for themselves. A few weeks ago, I would have been skeptical, but then look at what they did with my raft.

So that's the situation. A lot of places from around the country and the world are talking about how to send aid to Miami, but no one is really sure of the details yet. Some nonprofits are starting to work on it, but they have to be sure not to make the situation worse by getting the food to the wrong place, or getting looted, or other problems.

The bigger question that not enough people are asking — even now, with the city underwater — is what the new Miami will be like. So many are thinking in terms of temporary fixes: get some food to survivors, find homes for the refugees, and so on. That's important, but we also need to think about permanent changes.

What will the new Miami be like? The boats will have to become permanent. That's a given. They will have to distribute food and supplies by boats instead of trucks. They will have to find ways to get water and power to people without fixing the old systems. Because you can't fix those anymore. They're underwater now.

I wonder what the new Miami will be like. Only time will tell. In the meantime, all that we can do is watch it all unfold and send along our prayers and whatever help we can offer.

INTEGRAL ECOLOGY INITIATIVE
June 22, 2030 at 14:03

What a busy weekend! I've started my part-time job canvassing for a green group called the Integral Ecology Initiative. They work out of an office at Gaia House. They're not like any other nonprofit I've worked with before. They're a multidisciplinary academic center, but they also get involved in activist projects. They teach classes, publish research papers, and do what they can to help the community and region work on its relationship with the environment.

The canvassing they have me doing is really interesting. When I first heard about it, I thought it would be like what I did in other places: getting members for a nonprofit, getting candidates on the ballot, and so on. I used to do a lot of petitioning like that for the Green Party back when they weren't as established yet. But IEI is more about gathering information and using it to come up with new ideas and solutions. They do surveys, they do open-ended questionnaires, they even sometimes do less traditional things like a little play in the street where all of the people walking by become participants.

As soon as I told the guy that I was fresh off the train from Miami, his eyes lit up. Miami is really big in the news now in the U.S. and all over the world. There are a lot of major cities slowly sinking beneath the waves, but Miami is the hot topic now because Hurricane Florence is still so recent and they're still figuring out what to do about it. So this guy got excited and told me that he'd like me to do some surveys about Miami. He also wants me to speak at an event about my experiences in Miami. They're organizing a panel discussion with me as the Miami voice and several other people talking about the climate, the economy, and so on.

So I spent a few hours canvassing Friday night and another few hours this morning. I'll be going one more time tomorrow. It's not great money, even by southern Illinois standards. But it's a job doing something I love, which is talking to people about green issues and Miami.

I also spent some time out with Alejandra last night. We went salsa dancing and danced with a bunch of the college boys who are still in town for the summer. Most of them looked about ten years younger than me, but I didn't mind. Maybe they like me because I'm Alejandra's cousin, or maybe they like me because they've never met a Greek-Cuban girl before. Either way, they all wanted to dance with me. I'm okay with that.

But Alejandra wants to set me up with Ermete. I told her that I met Ermete at the food co-op and she told me what a great guy he is. She's always been such a matchmaker. She tries to set me up with guys because she only goes out with guys and wants me to find a good man to keep me happy. Honestly, though, I'm not looking for anything serious now. I just want to save up some money and get back to Miami, or someplace near Miami so I can volunteer on the weekends. But I'll humor her and spend some time with Ermete.

That's plenty of news for today. I've been reading the latest news from Miami, but I didn't see any major news over the last day or two. They're still debating a lot of the logistics and details of what to do next. Meanwhile, a few nonprofits have stepped in to fill in the gaps and meet some of the short-term needs of the people like food, water, safe shelter, and so on. This country would fall apart without the help of all of these volunteers and low-paid community organizers. God knows it's not the politicians or the corporations holding it all together as the temperatures rise and the oceans rise and everyone ends up broke and hungry and displaced. Anyway, I'll let you know if I hear anything new, especially if they don't talk about it on TV. I wouldn't be surprised if they gloss over all of the unpleasant details and make it seem like everything's fine in Miami.

BLUEBERRIES AND GREENS
June 24, 2030 at 23:12

I had a great weekend. After all of that canvassing, Alejandra invited me and a few of her friends to go pick some blueberries. It was really fun and the blueberries were so delicious! Ever since she moved from Chicago to southern Illinois for school, she's been doing all types of rural things like that.

It reminded me of all of my mom's stories about labor organizing with the migrant workers. Except in this case, it was just picking blueberries for an hour rather than all day, and we could work at our own pace. I can't even imagine how people work all day in that heat. I like going on outdoor adventures, but working outside all day in hot and muggy weather seems like a bad idea. No wonder they were always fighting for more pay and better conditions. They deserved it. And they still do.

We didn't spend too much time out there in the hills because it was over 100 degrees and high humidity. Also, Alejandra says the prices have gone up again this year due to another summer drought. So we didn't want to pick more than we could pay for. But it was fun while it lasted. I spent a little time talking to Ermete, which was nice. I also talked to Alejandra's friend Jess for a long time. Mi prima knows a lot of charming and beautiful people!

In other news, Miami has been hit by another storm. It wasn't as bad as Florence but it did cause a lot of problems. Maybe it was for the best though because now people are taking the idea that Miami is permanently underwater seriously. This idea is obvious to me, but so many people are still in denial. How can a major U.S. city just be underwater for good? Nothing like that has ever happened before. We've had some hard times in coastal cities for most of my life, but this is the worst the U.S. has ever seen. Miami really is underwater.

It's been interesting for me to see how people in southern Illinois respond. Most of them have probably never been to Miami. But I go to the bars and restaurants with Alejandra and I hear all of these people talking about it. "How can this be happening? What can we do? This has to be global warming. Why haven't they made fossil fuels illegal yet? We have to do something."

These are all good questions. It's good that people as far away as Illinois are this upset about what's going on in Miami. I'm really excited about the panel discussion on Wednesday. We can start coming up with some serious answers to these questions.

I'm a little nervous about it though because I found out that there will be a speaker from the Green Front on the panel. That means everything will be much more dangerous. Homeland Security will have people there. Those crazy anti-green militias might show up. I don't know what the ones in Illinois are called, but I'm sure they're at least as crazy as the ones in Florida. There might be arguments, fistfights, loaded weapons, people getting arrested. But I'm still going to speak. I'm not Green Front, so they can't arrest me just for talking about Miami. Not yet, anyway. And my mother was a community organizer, so I'm not going to let anyone bullying me into staying silent. I'm not very political, so this is the first time I've been on a panel like this. But I will say what I have to say about Miami. They can complain, but they can't stop me.

I may not post tomorrow because I'll be continuing the job search and meeting with a few more of Alejandra's friends for dinner. Maybe I'll post something small if I have time before bed. Either way, you can be sure that I'll post something after the meeting on Wednesday, even if it's very short. That way you'll know that I wasn't captured by Homeland Security or the anti-green militias. I say that jokingly, but only half jokingly. Wish me luck.

THE DISCUSSION
June 26, 2030 at 23:14

¡Dios mío! What a circus that was. Let me explain what happened.

They knew that the audience for the panel discussion would be too big for Gaia House, so they had it at the local university, SIU. The edge of campus is just across the street from Gaia House anyway, so it wasn't very far away. When I got to the ballroom where the panel discussion was scheduled, they were busy removing the partition walls that were dividing the room because they needed to add more seating!

Nobody had any idea just how big this would be. It felt like the entire town was there. There must have been about seven hundred people. It seemed like a concert, not a panel discussion. It really took some effort to walk past them all and go on stage.

Most of the people who came were just ordinary audience members. They were very talkative, had a lot of questions, and so on, but they were mostly just audience members. But then there were all of the other factions.

There was a group of about a dozen people who I can only assume were Homeland Security. They had black body armor, helmets, assault rifles, all of it. They never said who they were, but nobody else would have been allowed on campus with that kind of gear. Not even Bastion. They stood at the edges and just watched quietly, weapons at the ready, while a man and a woman in suits and holsters were circulating and recording some video and audio.

Then there was the Green Front section. People talk about them like it's one group, but it's actually about a dozen groups. A lot of people consider them to be terrorists, but they just seemed like ordinary people to me. There were a few dozen of them who were obvious and probably dozens more who just blended in with the crowd. The obvious ones were mostly young, although a few were middle-aged or elderly. They all tended to cluster together, and the young ones tended to wear green and black. Outside of the ballroom, they were rowdy and talkative, telling people all about climate change and the evils of fossil fuels and how we need a revolution today. But inside the ballroom, they were much more quiet, like they didn't want to get arrested or shot. They seem hot-headed at times, but they know how these things work.

People debate whether the Green Front are really terrorists. It's complicated. Who counts as Green Front? Where's the line between protest and insurrection? The government considers them terrorists but usually doesn't arrest them unless they're currently committing a crime. Sometimes they round up the organizers on conspiracy charges simply for supporting Green Front. But usually the government is more subtle than that. Instead, they observe, infiltrate, disrupt, cause chaos. They arrest people a few at a time, often in the middle of the night, often for unrelated charges. Maybe you didn't pay your parking tickets, or maybe you pirated movies, or maybe you have a late library book. They'll get you for that. I mean honestly, one time it really was for late library fees, although admittedly that woman owed a few hundred dollars. I guess she went underground and never returned her books.

Green Front can get away with being seen in public because there are so many of them. For a while, the government just arrested people who talked like they do. But now it's too many for the government to throw them all in prison, although they try. Honestly, it's even more people if you count everyone who votes for the new political parties — Green Party, Climate Party, and some of the smaller ones. If you count them as Green Front, that's at least a quarter of the population right there, maybe more. A few of them are even in the government now. Most people nowadays know we need to stop using fossil fuels, even if it takes some of the militant tactics like blocking roads, occupying land, damaging property, and so on. So they might all count as Green Front too.

Me, I try not to be political or militant like that. I don't want to go to prison. I just want to vote and leave it at that. But not these people. They keep pushing. The politicians don't like it, but they have to listen.

Anyway, speaking of listening, they eventually started the panel discussion. There was a climatologist, an economist, an engineer, a social scientist, the Green Front woman, and me, the refugee from Miami. I was most interested in the climatologist and engineer, but the crowd had the most questions for me and the Green Front woman.

Especially me. I talked for about fifteen minutes and the crowd was very engaged. They were always either listening in absolute silence or making a lot of noise when I said something intense. I've never spoken in front of that many people before, so it was exciting and scary and kind of amazing. Then at the end, they had the most questions for me. What was it really like in Miami? Did I think it would ever recover? Is it time for a revolution? That was a hard one. I told them I'm not political, but they just laughed. It's getting harder and harder these days to stay out of trouble.

There were a few crazy moments in there. Campus security had to remove several people who interrupted the panel. One was this crazy person who believed global warming was all a conspiracy. He got really angry, wouldn't stop talking, and actually tried to rush the stage. I don't know which one of us he wanted to strangle first, but the audience held him back. Then campus police took him away.

And then there were the militias — anti-green and pro-green. I didn't really notice the pro-green militia at first because they were quiet and blended in a bit with the (other?) Green Front people. But then about halfway through the panel discussion, about a dozen men in full camo stormed into the room with rifles in hand and started barking about the Second Amendment and how they had every right to participate in this forum without surrendering their weapons. They had been protesting outside, but I guess they got impatience and decided to push the boundaries and see if they could get away with going inside.

That was such a scary situation. As soon as the anti-green militia burst in the room, about a dozen pro-green militia men and women all stood up in unison and drew their concealed weapons. They were also in camo but they all had green armbands and a few other markings. The Homeland Security people in body armor raised their weapons too and made the anti-green militia stop near the doors. The one Homeland Security woman in a suit calmly but firmly explained to both militias that the law allowed them to carry weapons in public, but not on university property without express written permission.

It was intense for a while. The anti-green leader ranted and raved. He was so hostile. I don't know how he managed to avoid getting shot. A woman from the pro-green militia said they would leave if the others left. Eventually, the anti-green leader stormed out. After that, almost everybody with a weapon (other than Homeland Security) left the room. A few people from each faction passed their weapons to their friends and stayed inside for the question and answer period.

Amazingly, there was no actual violence. I thought that there would at least be a fistfight, but there was nothing, unless of course you count the crazy climate denier being firmly lead out of the room by campus police.

The panel lasted almost two hours and the questions lasted just as long. The general consensus among panelists and audience alike seemed to be that Miami is now permanently underwater, that other areas need to plan for similar fates, and that we all need to stop using fossil fuels immediately. At first people were hesitant to come out and say it because there was Homeland Security there, and people recording, and saying such things basically implies that you're Green Front. But people got up their courage, and no one got arrested, and the questions lead to several new ideas for how to respond to the situation. So all in all, it was a good night.

Thank God it's all over though. When it all ended, Alejandra could tell I was done talking for the night. She just took me home, made me a mojito, and set me down in front of the computer to write. She knows me so well. Now that I've finally got it all written down, though, it's time for some sleep. There's a lot of work to do and I want to be ready for it.

TRIP TO ST. LOUIS
June 29, 2030 at 23:24

After the crazy week I had, Alejandra decided that I needed a getaway. So she invited me to come with her to St. Louis for Friday and Saturday to visit a few of her old friends from college. We just got back a few minutes ago, so I want to write about it while it's fresh in my mind.

What a wonderful idea! It would have never occurred to me because I don't own a car. The bus and train are so expensive and difficult to deal with. But Alejandra has an old Tesla that she picked up used a few years ago when she had more money, so she can afford a trip like this every once in a while.

I feel sorry for all of these people in southern Illinois who still have to buy gas. Even with grid power prices going up every year, it's still cheaper to charge an electric than it is to fill a gas tank. Electrics are very affordable nowadays, but people in poor areas are often stuck with gas cars because so many people who want to stop using gas are desperate to sell them. They get an old used gas guzzler for cheap, but then they have to pay so much in fuel and repairs that they can never save up for electric. It's a vicious cycle. It's like those pay day loan places that give poor people a loan but then charge them so much interest that they never get out of debt.

Anyway, the trip to St. Louis was so good for me! On the drive up there, we were talking and laughing and singing along to the radio like two carefree teenagers again. We didn't even talk about Miami or the panel discussion or any of that. We just had a good ride through the country.

When we got to St. Louis, it was a little more serious. We did do some things just for fun, like seeing a play in the park with her friends and walking down the Delmar Loop for some food and shopping. But then we went to a small discussion about Miami that a local nonprofit was organizing.

This one wasn't nearly as crazy as the one in Carbondale. It was a small one that Alejandra heard about from her friends. There were only about three dozen people and most of them were actually refugees from Miami. We talked for hours about our problems, what it was like to leave Miami, when we planned to go back, and so on. Most of us do plan to go back, but we have different ideas of what that means. Some just want to live there again someday once Bastion has left and people have figured out the best ways to adjust to the new water levels. Others want to go back sooner to do relief work for all the brave souls who are still there trying to find food and water and power. Some stores and relief groups are starting to get food shipments in by boat, but they're still working out the details of how to make this a permanent rather than temporary arrangement.

It was a really good discussion and a really good trip. Even though I spent the afternoon talking about such a serious topic, it still felt like part of the vacation for me. I got to visit a real city again, I got to meet other refugees from Miami, and I got to spend the whole weekend with Alejandra and her friends. It was definitely a good way to spend the weekend.

I'm tired from the trip and need to get some sleep. Next time, though, I'll talk more about the latest news from Miami. After that conversation with the other refugees, and what happened in Miami on Friday, I'm sure I'll have a lot to say.

THE OCEAN CITY RESOLUTION
June 30, 2030 at 20:45

As you probably know by now, while I was off in St. Louis having a good time with Alejandra, big things were happening in Miami. The most important thing, of course, was the Ocean City Resolution.

What is the Ocean City Resolution? Why is it so important?

The Ocean City Resolution is Miami's way of saying that there's no going back to the way things were. Depending on how the rest of hurricane season goes, the waters may recede for a while. There may be a few awkward years where large parts of the city go above or below water based on how bad the storms get. But ultimately, there's no going back. Rather than spending the next few years fighting the inevitable, they have decided to accept that the city is in the ocean now.

This is apparently a big surprise to a lot of people, especially people outside of Miami. Personally, I don't find it too surprising. The latest version of the Southeast Florida Regional Climate Change Action Plan includes the concept of an ocean city and describes some general details about what it is, when it's time to declare yourself an ocean city, and so on. Green groups and some of the cities and counties have been preparing for this in their own way for decades. But people on TV don't talk about it, so I guess nobody knew about it, especially outside of southeast Florida.

People are going crazy about it. There are people out in the streets in every city talking about it, but they don't all agree on what to do. A lot of the politicians, and especially the people on Fox News, are saying some hateful things about us and telling us how to run our city. They say that Miami is a symbol. They say that we have a responsibility to show our fellow Americans and our enemies abroad that we are a strong, bold, resourceful people who will rise to the challenge. They say that by surrendering to the ocean, we are turning Miami from a symbol of America's strength to a symbol of America's decline.

But Miami is not a symbol. Miami is a city. Miami is a living, breathing organism, a real city full of real history and culture. I don't even know how to describe it. It's like asking a fish to describe the water it swims in. The scent of the ocean air has always been a part of my experience of Miami. You almost forget it sometimes when you're indoors. But then you go outside anywhere near the ocean and there it is. It's a salty scent that mingles with the trees and the sand, the bright colors of our city and our art, the city lights at night, the Cuban beats dancing through the streets, mojitos y cafecitos, proud people working hard and playing hard, real families making their way in the world, working for a better life, finding the American dream in our own way, our own place, the place we've come a long way to call home.

A place called Miami.

Miamians need to do what's good for Miami. And what's good for Miami is to accept the realities we face. If we keep fighting the rising tides, we will waste billions of dollars — and probably thousands of lives — on a strategy that is doomed to failure. Instead, we must adapt to our present and future circumstances. We must roll with the punches. To overcome this challenge, we must reinvent ourselves. We must accept that we are an ocean city now and do what we can to be the best ocean city that we can be.

In practical terms, this means a lot of hard work. Now that the City Commission has passed this resolution, we can begin the real work of adapting to the new realities of global warming. There are already plans on file for how to transition our water, our power, our internet, and our transportation to the realities of an ocean city. It will just take some time to assess how practical these plans are and implement them as best as we can with limited resources and time working against us.

On the bright side, there may also be some incredible opportunities. If the city can find the money for it, and if the insurance companies actually pay up on all of those policies, there will be a lot of jobs rebuilding the infrastructure to be compatible with the conditions in an ocean city. There's also growing speculation that some of the big property owners will simply cut their losses and abandon their properties or sell their properties for pennies on the dollar. It's just not worth it for them to pay large sums of money to repair and renovate properties that will probably never be half as profitable as they were just a few weeks ago. Who knows what will happen to these properties. Maybe the banks will take them, or maybe the squatters will keep them, or maybe something no one predicted will happen. Who knows.

This Ocean City Resolution and all of the related news makes me really want to go back to Miami. But I need to be practical and responsible about it. I need to replace some of the money and supplies that I used up or abandoned getting out of Miami. Since Alejandra is letting me stay here for free, I can probably do that in just another month or two. Then when I'm ready, I can go back home.

In the meantime, I wish the best of luck to those who are still in the city. You are in my thoughts and prayers every day. I look forward to seeing you again soon.

THE SOLUTIONS PROJECT
July 2, 2030 at 14:26

Rumors are circulating about another big announcement coming out of Miami later this week. If my sources are right, it won't be good news. Therefore, I'd like to spend today talking about something positive. Mostly positive, anyway.

The Solutions Project is a visionary effort to accelerate the transformation of U.S. energy infrastructure to 100% clean and renewable energy. Back in the early teens, they brought together a team of scientists, business people, and activists in order to develop detailed plans for each state to make the transition. It included a suggested balance of clean energy types, several options for how to go about making it happen, and so on.

It was brilliant, really. That was exactly what so many people needed at the time. One of the main excuses that all of the politicians and fossil fuel barons were using was the whole "it's not ready" argument. "Oh, solar is okay in theory, but it's not ready yet. Maybe in ten years." And then ten years later, they would say the same thing. So the politicians would let fossil fuels get away with all types of murder, while at the same time they would fight tooth and nail to keep solar and wind from getting more established.

The Solutions Project united people from different disciplines and different ideological perspectives behind a clear, simple, attainable goal. "Here's the technology; here's the economics; here's the policy. Let's do this."

In a way, they were successful in their goal. They definitely accelerated the change. Business people took it as a guide for how they should develop their businesses. Activists used it as a resource every time some fool opened their mouth and said it wasn't possible. When a growing number of Greens and Climaters and clean Republicrats got elected, they used the policy guidelines to help encourage the change. Solutions Project gave all of these people hope and did a lot of the legwork so that each local group or campaign wouldn't have to reinvent the wheel every time they wanted to advocate for clean energy. It was an exciting time, and really I think it changed the political landscape almost as much as it changed the energy landscape. Which is a lot.

Sadly, as you may have noticed, they didn't reach 100% by 2030. There are a few states that have reached a 99% rating, which basically means that all power generated within the state is clean and all vehicles directly owned by the government are clean. But some states aren't even at 50%, and even the 99% states still technically use fossil fuels in some ways — grid connection to dirtier states, or a bunch of smelly gas guzzling cars and trucks, things like that.

Even so, it was a valiant effort. It changed the way that we think about energy in this country. It also change the way that a lot of states get their energy.

And the work continues. On January 1, they announced their new goal of 100% clean energy nationwide by 2040. Then on the weekend of the Summer Solstice, the longest day of the year, they had a big event at the MREA Energy Fair up in Wisconsin to announce the release of their new and improved plan.

It's not perfect, but it's something. I'll admit that I was a little depressed in January when we didn't hit 100%. But other than that, it's been very inspiring, and it continues to inspire change for the better. In the midst of all these problems, we need to remember our inspirations. Otherwise, we'll get paralyzed by fear and grief and do nothing. So let's focus on the solutions that make the most sense and do what we can to make them a reality.

FRIENDS, FIREWORKS, AND INSURANCE
July 5, 2030 at 14:31

I had a good Fourth of July yesterday. I went to watch the fireworks here in town with Alejandra, Jess, Ermete, and a few friends from Gaia House. I always enjoy the fireworks, but somehow having friends and family with you turns it into more of an experience.

Alejandra was mostly just quiet during the show, which is funny because she's usually such a talker. She gets that way sometimes when we're out at a show, whether it's a movie, music, a play, whatever. She loses herself in it. She gets this look of awe in her eyes and just looks and listens and experiences it all. Ermete, on the other hand, is a science nerd. He was talking about how fireworks used to be more toxic and produce more smoke until the regulations made them greener. That got Jess started talking about how it was still so wasteful when we haven't even stopped CO_2 emissions from power plants and vehicles yet. But then she admitted that it was beautiful and started making all types of jokes about random things from TV and movies. She insisted that it was the end of the world and the fireworks were part of some type of real battle. But we couldn't decide if it was a zombie apocalypse, or a climate apocalypse, or maybe an alien invasion that we were fighting off with colorful smiley face explosions.

Sometimes it's good to talk about normal things like that for a while. But I really should get back to the latest news from Miami.

When I woke up this morning, I was just hoping to have a nice, calm, quiet day to recover from staying up late having a few drinks with new friends. But then I turn on my phone and the first thing I see is a headline about the insurance companies.

For the past few weeks, everyone has been holding their breaths as the property and casualty insurance companies assess the damages in Florida. It's been almost a month since Hurricane Florence made landfall, so in theory, they should have said and done much more by now. But so far they've done almost nothing. So rumors have been spreading that there were all sorts of threats and arguments going on behind closed doors between the insurance companies, the reinsurers, the state and federal agencies, and the big property owners. We may never know all the details, but we do know the outcome.

Nobody is going to pay for the damages from Hurricane Florence.

Of course, it's all going to be fought out in the courts. The property owners will sue the private and public insurers for not paying. The insurers will sue various governments and possibly corporations for not doing enough to prepare for climate change. The government may put the companies into receivership, liquidate their assets, who knows what else. Meanwhile, all of the TV and internet pundits are doing their best to explain the complexities of insurance regulations and agencies.

Some people in the insurance industry have made public statements explaining the situation in simpler terms. The simple version is that regardless of who wins what court cases, there's no way anybody is going to get insurance money unless there's a major government bailout of the entire industry, something like the bank bailout of 2008. But this would cost more money than that, and the state and federal governments are way more broke now than they were in 2008, so it's not likely to happen.

What does this mean for Miami? Mostly bad, bad news.

Over the past couple of decades, Miami has already seen some people and businesses leave because of the cost of insurance. You basically have a choice between very expensive private insurance or cheaper public insurance that doesn't have enough money to pay your claims unless it gets a public bailout. So people in coastal areas throughout Florida and up the whole East Coast have been either leaving or struggling under the weight of heavy insurance premiums and rebuilding costs.

Thing have gradually been getting worse. Everyone outside of the Tea Party knows that it's because of global warming. But this is the straw that broke the camel's back. Hurricane Florence has left large parts of the city more or less uninhabitable. Even the places that didn't really get damaged in the storm need renovations so that they can get updated water and power systems as well as first floor designs that can take on water without being damaged.

That takes money. And without any help from the insurance companies or the government, even some of the most elite properties in Miami don't have enough money lying around to do such major repairs and renovations. The ones that do are smart enough to know that it may not be worth it. Will they ever turn a profit again if they have a five star hotel but the city has become a ghost town?

Some people are saying it's not as bad as it seems. Every crisis is an opportunity. Maybe something good will come of the fact that property values in Miami are dropping to the lowest levels since the city was founded.

But it doesn't feel that way. It feels like just when Miamians are starting to pull together and rebuild the city, all the politicians and corporations have let us down. With just a little help, we could have such a great recovery. There are all of these great plans developing for how to rise to the challenge and adapt to the situation. But corporations and governments alike have decided it's not worth the risk or the trouble. They just want to let Miami be overrun with toxic floodwaters and decaying buildings and rampant crime and out-of-state mercenaries whose idea of law and order is to rob and terrorize the people they're supposed to protect.

Before all this happened, I never really knew how much Miami meant to me. It was just the place I lived, you know? But now more than ever, I know that I have to go back there and do something about this. I'm not a political person, but to me, this isn't political. This is helping the city I grew up in, the place I call home, recover from a disaster.

I have a few ideas. Other people do too. It's going to take some time and some organizing, but we can do it. If the insurance companies all go bankrupt, and the government won't help, then we'll do it our own way. This is bad news, but we'll make the most of it. We'll make Miami livable for everyone who stayed there and everyone who makes it back there in the next few months. I'm sure of it.

MIAMI MEETUPS
July 8, 2030 at 17:20

What a busy weekend! Since it was a holiday weekend, I thought I would just hang out with Alejandra and relax. But between the news from Miami and the long conversations with Jess and Ermete, I was feeling restless. So I found plenty to keep me busy.

First of all, I have some good job news. I may be able to do some part time solar installation and energy efficiency work. I did similar work when I was fresh out of college, so I had the experience and training they were looking for. It's not a permanent position, just me providing an extra pair of hands when big jobs come up or their full-time staff are too busy. For me, though, that's perfect. It's good work, it pays well, and when I'm ready to move back to Miami, I can just go without finding a replacement. No big deal.

I've also been talking to a big group of Miamians online called the Miami Diaspora. It's mostly Miami refugees like me, but it also includes some Miamians who are still in the city and have internet access. We want to organize a national conference as soon as possible, but we're thinking it should be online for a variety of obvious reasons like transportation costs, wanting it to be a carbon neutral event, etc. So we may just have a Miami Meetup in a few major cities with some telepresence rooms set up to give it the look and feel of a face-to-face conference.

On top of all that, ever since that panel discussion, I've had a growing number of local people talk to me about the situation in Miami. It started with one or two community organizers, but now it includes teachers, students, a few business people, even someone on the local city council. Jess and Ermete are both very active in the community, so they put me in touch with more people over the weekend. Most of it has been on the phone or online because it was a weekend, but Jess is going to take me to a meeting with some of her friends tomorrow.

There are a handful of other Miami refugees here in Carbondale, but so far I'm the only one who's gone public, so people have a lot of questions for me. I'm starting to feel like an unofficial Miami ambassador. People are starting to recognize me on the street when I walk by. It's strange. It reminds me of when I was growing up and my mom would have all these people calling her, texting her, visiting her, and so on because she was an organizer. Sometimes it was annoying, but as I got older, I respected her for it. She didn't always know what to do, but she tried. I wish she were still around today to give me some advice, but she passed away while I was in college.

The closest Miami Meetup will probably be in St. Louis. In the meantime, there's plenty to do locally. I've been very happy to see all of these people in southern Illinois who are connecting the dots between Miami and global warming. There are a lot of people here who are really eager to do something about global warming. You wouldn't expect it at first because sometimes the culture feels like the South, especially outside of Carbondale. And we all know how some people in the South are still fighting the green economy, against all odds and common sense. But they have a long tradition of environmental advocacy in southern Illinois. Jess told me a little bit about it and it was really interesting.

Community leaders here are drawing connections between Miami and all of the droughts, floods, and incredible heat they experience locally. Everyone around here is worried about how global warming is ruining local agriculture. So when you add Miami on top of that, it's the straw that broke the camel's back. And it's an election year, so there are all of these heated political debates too. Sometimes it feels like a pressure cooker, everyone ready to just burst into a rant about something or other related to the climate, the elections, and so on.

Anyway, I've got to go eat some dinner and go to another meeting. I'll post again soon with any news about local organizing or the Miami Meetups.

SOUTHERN ILLINOIS 350
July 10, 2030 at 14:57

The worst thing about global warming is chocolate. When I was growing up, you could buy a small candy bar made with real chocolate for only a dollar or two. Now the same candy bars — the cheapest milk chocolate ones! — cost at least ten dollars. The good ones cost almost twenty. I miss cheap coffee too, but everybody complains about that. Most people don't make a serious complaint about chocolate because it's seen as a luxury. But for some of us, it's a way of life. And now thanks to global warming, chocolate crops are really suffering. It will never be as cheap as it was when I was a kid.

¡Dios mío! That makes me feel so old. Is thirty two old? Anyway, I didn't come on here to talk about chocolate. I have other news.

I met with three of Jess' friends yesterday. They're part of Southern Illinois 350, a coalition of local people and groups that take various actions in response to climate change. They were up at the Energy Fair in Wisconsin a couple of weeks ago and saw the keynote speech given by Hakima Althea from the Solutions Project.

As you've probably noticed, her speech went viral. If you haven't seen it for some reason, go watch it now.

Solutions Project isn't really a protest group, and Hakima Althea usually isn't a protest speaker. I saw her talk in person once in Miami and watched a few of her videos online. She's a very level-headed electrical engineer who speaks very calmly but very firmly about how important it is to switch to clean energy and how easy it is from a technological perspective. People like her because she makes it all seem so clear and reasonable and possible.

Nobody was expecting her to give the speech that she gave.

At the beginning, she spent about two minutes giving her usual speech about the technology. Renewables are ready. But then she went on this big, impassioned, visionary rant about how we need to deploy all of our psychological, social, economic, and political technologies to shut down the fossil fuel industry and replace it all with clean energy. She mentioned Miami and talked about how every city in the world is going to go through its own "Miami moment" within the next few decades. She emphasized that the remaining fossil fuel industry was only benefiting a "handful of people in a handful of countries" and that the rest of the world was "on the cusp of apocalyptic changes" as a result of their greed. She urged everyone to do what they can to prepare their communities and their countries for these disasters. But most of all, she said that people in the U.S. and a few other "hyper-emitters" had a "moral responsibility to shut down the fossil fuels industry by any means necessary".

The response has been tremendous. The video is already on track to being one of the most viewed and liked videos on YouTube. It probably will be by the end of the month. Green Front militias have pledged their support for her call to action and Tea Party militias are calling her a terrorist and calling for her capture and execution as an enemy combatant. None of that really surprises me, though. What surprises me is the number of people in the middle who support her. People these days are afraid of getting harassed or arrested for reading the wrong books, visiting the wrong websites, talking to the wrong people. But they watch her video, they like it, they talk about it at work, and so on. Maybe it's precisely because she was just a mild-mannered electrical engineer who was much more level-headed until her sister was displaced by Hurricane Florence.

I've watch that video about a dozen times by now. It's amazing. I sometimes put it on in the morning and listen to it while I get ready to remind myself what I need to be doing with my life now.

So when Jess' friends saw this speech in Wisconsin, they decided to do something local here in Illinois. They're starting up the local branch of a statewide campaign to get the entire State of Illinois to use 100% clean renewable energy by 2040. It's been tried before, back when the Solutions Project was just getting started and the goal was 100% by 2030. But they feel very optimistic about it this time. There are actually a few Greens and Climaters in the state assembly now, so they know they can at least get a few bills on the table. The problem will be applying pressure to force the more conservative politicians — the Democrats, the Republicans, maybe even the lone Libertarian — to vote in favor of clean energy policies.

I've decided to help them. They wanted someone from Miami who can talk about the situation there and how it relates to Illinois. They also just need more hands for things like canvassing, organizing events, and other things. Most of it won't be paid work, but I might get paid for a few things, and I won't let it interfere with my paid work. So it seems like a good idea to me. It's funny, though, how I was a lot less political when I was living in a big city. Now I live in a small town in a rural area and everybody wants me to do some organizing!

I still have a few more things to do today, but tomorrow is going to be my day off. Which is good because they have these big free concerts in Carbondale every Thursday. The music is hit or miss but it's fun to go to the park and meet all these people and listen to music in the background. Jess tends to get political and go around talking to people about her projects, but I tend to just relax and be social. Ermete and Alejandra actually sit and listen to the music. It's a good time, but I wish it weren't so hot and humid! There are always heat advisories, a few cooling tents, an ambulance on stand-by, and so on. I can mostly set aside politics when I'm out at a concert, but when I have to go to the cooling tent to cool off, I can't help but think of global warming.

But I don't let it get to me. I need some time to just relax with friends, otherwise I'll go insane. So I just laugh, shake my head, and get back to the concert. I need to enjoy this life while it lasts.

SLOW AND STEADY
July 12, 2030 at 22:20

Slow and steady wins the race, or so they say. I feel eager to get back to Miami, and so many people locally and globally feel eager to do something dramatic about global warming. But I must be strategic about this, and we must be strategic about this. One thing at a time.

Thursday was a carefree day, just as I hoped it would be. I ran some errands with Alejandra, did some reading, had dinner with Jess, went to the concert, and watched some TV with Jess and Ermete. Since Jess was involved, we couldn't help talking about politics and Miami a little bit, but it was a very fun and relaxing day off.

Today was a busy day. I spent some time at Gaia House volunteering in the garden with a woman named Dharani. It's been another rough year for gardeners and farmers in Southern Illinois, but they know by now that they need to do everything possible to prepare for droughts and floods. It's amazing that they have so much food growing there in these conditions. While we worked out in the garden, we listened to a community radio station called WDBX. Nobody had the radio on the last time I volunteered in the garden, but Dharani wanted to listen to a local environmental talk show, so she turned it on for a while. As you can imagine, the main topics were global warming and Miami.

Later in the day, I did some paid canvassing for Integral Ecology Initiative and Southern Illinois 350. Gardening in the morning wasn't too bad, but walking around with a clipboard in that mid-day heat and humidity was too much. I had to take breaks and drink plenty of water. I got a lot of signatures for the new clean energy petition, though, so it was worth it.

The news doesn't really talk about this organizing. At least not the big corporate shows and sites. If that's where you get your news, you wouldn't even know that there are people in every state who are out in the streets on a daily basis to gather petitions, raise funds, and get the word out about Miami and global warming and what we can do about it. There's some debate among organizers about what the next big thing should be, but everyone knows that big things are coming.

I didn't even realize it until I started doing this canvassing. I thought this was just important to me because I'm from Miami and I've cared about global warming all my life. But almost everybody wants to do something now. People see me with a clipboard and I don't even have to walk up to them. They walk up to me and ask me what they can do, what they can sign, where the next meeting is. There are still people who blow me off or say rude things, but it's so rare now compared to when I did this a few years ago.

People want change. They know it'll take time, but they're restless, looking for solutions to all of the problems that global warming has caused. I don't know the answers any more than the next person, but I'm glad I can help everyone get organized. If we all put our heads together, and do the hard work that needs to be done, we'll get there eventually. I just hope we get it done before any more cities go underwater.

JESS AND ERMETE
July 14, 2030 at 20:09

I've been spending a lot of time with Jess and Ermete lately. I'll probably be spending even more time with them soon as some of this organizing heats up. So I may as well tell you a little more about them.

Jess is hard to describe. She grew up in Southern Illinois and has spent most of her life here, so she knows all about the history, the people, the land, and so on. On that level, it's obvious that she's a local. But on another level, you would think she came here from some big city. She's very intelligent and very talkative when there's a political or philosophical discussion. She has all of these big green political ideas that she talks about in great detail with anyone who will listen. The way she talks so quickly and passionately and intellectually about politics reminds me of one of my New York organizer friends. Usually the locals here with those types of beliefs are slow to talk about them with new people because they don't want to be labeled Green Front. That's a good way to get run out of town in some parts of Southern Illinois. But Jess has no hesitation. She just says what's on her mind. She's not rude about it, but she also doesn't care if it offends you. She's very outspoken. I like that about her.

Ermete is a bit more soft-spoken. He's also very intelligent, as you may have guessed from his interests in science and engineering. But he waits to see if you're interested in what he has to say. If you are, he'll lean in closer and tell you in hushed tones all about the secrets of the universe. As he talks, his eyes widen at the most exciting parts, and his hands trace shapes in sweeping gestures as if to show you the curving of magnetic fields, or the shape of molecules, or the structure of political systems. He's lived in the United States most of his life, but he was born in Italy and has a noticeable Italian accent. It's interesting. His voice has an almost musical quality to it.

They are both organizers at heart. Jess is a grad student in communication studies and Ermete finds odd jobs related to his green interests, especially anything technical. They have very different styles, but they both have these similar visions of how to improve their community, and they both spend a lot of time and energy making it happen. Even when the details are a little boring, the overall lifestyle is very exciting. I can see the appeal. I used to just do this type of thing in my spare time as my way of giving back to the community. But now I want to do more.

We hope to do a lot together while I'm here this summer. It will take some time to organize anything big, but there are plenty of small things to do in the meantime. There are times when I wish I had found a place to stay closer to Miami so that I could visit on the weekends and do some volunteering there. But then I would have missed out on spending the summer with Alejandra and meeting Jess and Ermete. At the end of the day, I think I made the right choice.

MIAMI LIVES
July 16, 2030 at 23:22

It's been a busy day, so I won't talk too long this time. But I do want to talk about some of the latest news from Miami.

The first thing is the humanitarian situation. No one is entirely sure just how many people are still living in and around Miami. The worst of the flooding only goes about as far north as Coral Springs and Boca Raton, but the whole metropolitan area is considered a disaster area because of the refugee crisis. All of the areas farther south are mostly underwater and mostly deserted. The areas farther north are packed with refugees.

The people left in the city are a strange mix. Some are too poor to get away. Some stayed to protect their property. Some work for social services. Some are police, National Guard, and so on. Some are criminals trying to take advantage. Some are activists trying to provide relief. Some are just ordinary people who see it as a dangerous but exciting adventure. Some are even tourists, if you can believe it. It's Miami, there will always be tourists.

There are also a lot of people from Bastion, although it's not entirely clear who's paying them since the city and state governments are too broke.

The poor people who stayed in the flooded areas often have to walk or swim through the water, which is not entirely safe or clean. People are getting sick, infected cuts, too much salt water, a few drownings, that type of medical trouble. If they have at least a few dollars, they can take the Green Boatbus, a nonprofit transport service with an electric motor, phone charging, solar power, and some water purification. At night, they have to find someplace to stay or at least hide, otherwise they will have to deal with the gangs or Bastion. Bastion's less likely to kill you, but just as likely to rob you. Some people think the stories are exaggerated, but they took my raft, so I know better.

More food and water is making it into the city now. There are some stores and makeshift aid distribution centers open for business. Some are on dry land and others are smaller operations that run out of a boat or the second floor of a flooded building. The Ocean City Resolution helped make a lot of this possible by giving the boats official permission to operate in the city and making it easier to do any type of business or relief work out of these boats during the transition period. It's still chaotic, but at least now there's new food coming in so most people don't have to loot abandoned stores and houses in order to survive.

None of that is entirely new, but more details are coming out as reporters, public officials, aid workers, and so on assess the situation. The biggest problem still seems to be the flooded sewage system. They did try to make some improvements before Hurricane Florence, but it wasn't enough. Some people never fully accepted the realities of the situation until it was too late. They had such a short-sighted mentality. When your city's not underwater yet, it's easy to say that there's no need to spend billions of dollars on new sewage systems. But then when you're city's underwater, it's too late, and you realize you should have done something sooner.

And your constituents realize it too. There are some tough elections coming up, I'm sure.

Anyway, the good news is that there are a lot of ideas and options. Most city and state officials didn't do nearly enough to prepare, but there were a few who paid attention, and some of the agencies and nonprofits made detailed plans for what to do when the city and state dropped the ball. There are also some activists and social entrepreneurs who see this as a major opportunity. The bottom has dropped out on the real estate market, so they can buy up properties for pennies on the dollar. Most people won't want to buy those properties because they're flooded, nobody wants to rent them, there's no working plumbing, and so on. But if you have some innovative idea for how to fix some of these problems facing the city, it may be the perfect deal for you.

If you know of any specific projects like that, please let me know about it. It would be great if some nonprofit or green business were hiring Miami refugees to go back to Miami and get some work done. I would take that opportunity in a heartbeat. I'll let you know how it goes. In the meantime, slow and steady.

CALL TO ACTION
July 19, 2030 at 13:36

Miami Diaspora, the online group of Miami refugees and people still living in Miami, has released their first call to action. Really, I should say our first call to action since I was on the committee. But I didn't do much, just talk about the ideas and let the writers in the group write the actual text. I did get to see the text a few hours before it was sent out to the media, which was fun.

This is the first public statement that Miami Diaspora has made. The original idea of the group was just to have an online discussion of our experiences of Hurricane Florence and maybe eventually a conference. It was a personal support network, both in the sense of talking about our personal stories and in the sense of supporting people who were looking for food, shelter, medical care, and so on. But it quickly became more than that. Since most people have left Miami, and some of us have gone to other cities, the best way for Miamians to keep in touch is online. Since we're the biggest group of Miamians online, it occurred to someone that we could be the unofficial voice of Miami.

And the voice of Miami should not remain silent.

The call to action asks people around the world to take action on global warming. It describes two broad strategies: the Resilience Program and the Resistance Program.

The Resilience Program is all about creating cities and states that are resilient enough to handle all of the changes caused by global warming. At this point, there's no going back. Global warming has already changed the world and will continue changing the world for the foreseeable future. We need to accept that these changes are real and do what we can to adapt. This means things like preparing for rising sea levels, floods, droughts, food shortages, diseases, all of these types of chaos caused by global warming. Each city has to figure out its own plan and follow through with it as soon as possible. Some cities are already doing this, but we need much more work like this. All the troubles in Miami today show what happens if you put it off too long.

The Resistance Program is definitely going to be more controversial, at least among some people. It says that the entire world needs to stop using fossil fuels by 2040 and calls on the people of the world to do everything they can to make the governments and corporations meet this deadline. They stopped just short of saying anything explicit that would get us all arrested as Green Front militants. But they did talk about things like protests, boycotts, divestment, and so on.

So many of our major cities — New York, Tokyo, London, hundreds of others — are right on the edge of the water. They're all starting to feel the effects. If the oceans keep rising, sooner or later, all of these cities will be underwater. We've seen it happen in places like the Maldives. Now it's knocking on our front door. Miami is underwater, and other major cities will be too within my lifetime.

This press release just went out a couple of hours ago, so we still haven't seen the full response yet. But it's already starting to show up on the corporate news shows. That's a pretty big deal since those shows seem to avoid talking about global warming whenever possible. They're owned by the same people who own the oil and gas companies, so of course they avoid talking about it. But this is so big and new that they can't help talking about it.

The call to action is open-ended. It describes what people should do about global warming in general from this point forward. But it also declares a global day of action on August 2. This is when we'll do the Miami Meetups, which is a project by some of the same organizers. It will also probably involve a Resilience event and a Resistance event in each city.

I've been talking to Jess and Ermete about this. We haven't decided yet if we're going to do something here in town or go to St. Louis for a bigger event. It may depend on what other people we know want to do. Alejandra's not very political, but she says she's up for something like this and she's fine with whatever we decide. We need her Tesla to get to St. Louis, so I'm glad she's willing to help. And I haven't been spending as much time with her lately, so a two hour road trip to St. Louis would be great.

That's definitely the biggest news today. I'll post again when I know more about our local plans for this day of action. In the meantime, Ermete has invited me to some type of trivia night fundraiser for Gaia House. I've never been to a trivia night, but it sounds fun and it's for a good cause. I'm still trying to save up money, but ten dollars for a trivia night is a good deal. I'm not really a trivia person though, so I hope I don't embarrass myself.

AUGUST 2
July 22, 2030 at 16:21

Happy Monday! As you may have noticed, everyone's been talking about the call to action from Miami Diaspora. Local people, internet people, TV people, even the President. Needless to say, I've had a busy weekend.

I don't have much experience as an organizer. My mom was an organizer, and I've done some work and volunteering for nonprofits — canvassing, cleanups, homeless outreach, that type of thing. But there's a big difference between showing up to an event and organizing an event. Lately, I've been learning all about the difference.

There are so many details to take care of! The devil's in the details. When other people in Miami Diaspora started talking about the Miami Meetups, I thought it would be very simple, at least for me. Carbondale isn't very big, so I thought I would just carpool to St. Louis with a few friends for the St. Louis meetup. But this call to action has everyone itching to get involved. So now we're having what is basically two conferences on the same weekend — the small Miami Meetups conference we originally planned and a big Miami Allies conference.

Carbondale is definitely big enough for Miami Allies. We had a few hundred people show up on campus just to hear a few speakers talk about the situation in Miami. Now we're going to have a global teleconference. I'm sure we'll get at least as many people for this one. And I don't even know what to do with them all. Which is bad news because Miami Diaspora has asked me to be the lead organizer!

I've never organized anything like this before. I feel like would be lost without Jess and Ermete here to help me get it done. Jess has put me in touch with a few people from Gaia House, the Integral Ecology Initiative, the Shawnee Green Party, and Southern Illinois 350 who are all eager to help. Ermete knows a few tech wizards who are just as eager to handle the telepresence aspect of the conference. There will be people here having old fashioned face-to-face meetings and conversations, but a lot of the action will involve using telepresence to connect us with people in other cities. Some organizers already do this on a small scale, but Ermete says that this may end up being the biggest town hall style teleconference ever. I guess we'll see. Everyone I meet is talking about this, so I wouldn't be surprised.

That's all I have time for at the moment. Now that we're planning a local Miami Ally event, there are so many details to consider — location, transportation, food, security, maybe even places to stay for people who live in the smaller towns around here and want to spend the whole weekend here. That's a tall order for two weeks, even for people like Jess and Ermete who have done stuff like this before. Alejandra has never really done anything like this either, so she's mostly just showing her support by reminding me to eat, sleep, and unwind every now and then. She's also letting me borrow the Tesla every now and then to run errands. I'm so lucky to have mi prima here for all of this!

I'll have more news soon, I'm sure. In the meantime, please, feel free to tell me what's going on in your part of the world. Are you organizing a Miami Meetup or a Miami Ally event? Do you live in Miami or somewhere else that's really hurting from the effects of global warming? Let me know!

MIAMI ALLIES IN CARBONDALE
July 25, 2030 at 01:05

It's been a busy week! I usually post about every other day, but this is the busiest I've been since relocating to Southern Illinois. Luckily, it's mostly been good news.

All of the details for the Miami Allies weekend here in Carbondale are coming together nicely. Some of the students at Gaia House were able to help me reserve a few different rooms on campus for local discussions and telepresence rooms to connect us with participants in other cities. I've used simple telepresence tools before, but they have some pretty advanced ideas they want to try.

Part of it involves stringing together small conference rooms from four or more cities together into a single virtual conference room. I've been to a meeting where they did that with two conference rooms, but if they can do what they have in mind, this will be so much bigger. They say it's going to offer some of the same excitement you get from having a huge international conference, but with a lot less travel and fossil fuel use involved, and a lot more inclusion of people who are low income, people who can't travel, disenfranchised people. These are people who often get excluded from huge conferences even when the organizers mean well. The way we're running it, any random person can walk in off the street for free and participate in this big conference about global warming and Miami with people from around the world. That is beautiful to me. I'm happy to have so many people here who are helping to make it happen.

The only bad news is that the anti-green militias are making trouble. There are several small militias around here who have formed a coalition. They say that the university is being taken over by Green Front and that everyone who shows up at the conference should be arrested for treason. They will be marching and protesting all weekend, probably with as many guns as they're legally allowed to carry, if not more.

This isn't even supposed to be a protest event, unless you count the one big permitted march that we're doing at the end just to demonstrate how many of us showed up to the event in each city. But they're turning it into a protest event. It reminds me of all the chaos at the panel discussion a while ago. I really don't like it.

And they won't be alone. There will also be a pro-green militia called the Green Guard. They openly identify as Green Front, but they're very careful about obeying the law, so they haven't been arrested or disbanded by the government. Not yet, anyway. They're actually fairly quiet and private, but they show up at times like this to make sure the anti-greens don't flip out and massacre everyone. The anti-greens aren't specifically threatening violence, but that one guy seemed very hot-headed at the panel discussion, so you never know.

As much as I tend to avoid guns myself, I do feel a little safer knowing that the Green Guard will be there. I just hope it all stays peaceful. This is all just about helping solve some serious problems in Miami and in the world. If people can keep their tempers and egos in check, everything else should go smoothly.

"GO HOME"
July 27, 2030 at 22:59

All of our planning for the big conference next weekend is going smoothly. Ermete and his friends are testing out some of the hardware and software for the telepresence rooms. Jess is talking to local community groups in and around Carbondale about the conference. For about a day, there was some concern about the rules for serving food from outside sources on campus. But then we found an administrator who helped us to get special permission because the food was all local and some of it came from an organic garden on campus. Now that most of my organizing work is done, I took some time off from all of that this weekend to help with a local solar installation.

It's been good to be busy again. I like to feel productive, so when I take a break from one thing, I just work on something else. Sometimes that adds up to a lot of work at the end of the week. But the change is refreshing. Just when I was getting tired of talking to people endlessly about global warming and Miami, I got to go up on a hot roof and help install some solar modules. It's hard sometimes because you have to focus on the technical details of the job while you're up there in the heat (or cold). But that's part of what I like about it. It's hard work, but it's good work, and I can lose myself in it for a whole day.

Of course, because everything else is going so well, something bad had to come up.

I've been getting these phone calls. I didn't know who it was at first because they would just call, listen, and hang up. It was a few different Southern Illinois numbers, but always the same behavior. Call, listen, hang up. Strange, but no big deal.

It was a much bigger deal when they started telling me to go home.

The first voice was a very male voice. I say very male because his voice was like gravel and about two octaves below mine.

"Go home!"

The second voice was a woman. She sound like she may have been an older woman.

"Go home you [blanking] [blank] [blank]!"

The third voice was a young man who spoke in a quiet but very stern tone of voice.

"Go home, green. You've been warned."

I honestly found that one the most disturbing. Not because of what he said, at least not entirely. It was because of the way he said it. He sounded angry, but also very disciplined. This wasn't some prank call made on a whim. This was serious.

Alejandra told me I should call the police. I wasn't sure. Whose side are the police on? What if they're the ones making the calls?

I eventually decided to call them. The woman I talked to seemed to take it seriously, but it sounded like nobody would be following up on it anytime soon. She also gave me the number of someone in Homeland Security, but honestly I don't know if I really want to go looking for trouble like that. It's just some phone calls. Probably just some locals who think they can scare me away with a few threatening phone calls.

They must not know me very well.

It's ironic because I do plan to "go home" to Miami eventually. But not because these bullies made an anonymous phone call. And if they mean "go home" as in get out of America, then they really need some educating. I'm just as American as they are. I was born in America, I grew up in America, and I'll probably die in America. This is my home too. And demanding that our politicians actually listen to the will of the people about things like global warming is very American of me too. More American than secretly threatening people on the phone because you disagree with them.

Anyway, I'm not trying to worry anybody. The main reason I'm mentioning it is to see if anyone else is getting these phone calls, or visits, or anything like that. I don't just mean in Southern Illinois, although that's important too. I mean anyone who's working on Miami or global warming or related issues. If you've had anything like this happen, let me know. And don't let them get you down. They're just scared because they know that most people want change and they're not ready for it.

MAY 8
July 31, 2030 at 12:10

I've been so busy getting ready for the conference that I haven't written as much lately. That's actually good news because I haven't had much to complain about! I did get two more of those strange rude phone calls, but everything else with the conference is going well. We have all the rooms reserved, all the technology is working, and hundreds of people have already registered. There are still some details to take care of, but it's really exciting to see it all come together so quickly.

Since that's all going well, I'm going to take a few minutes to tell you about the May 8 storm.

Jess was the first one to tell me about this storm. Ever since she told me, I've been reading all about it and looking at all the pics of the destruction. On May 8, 2009, there was an incredible storm that hit Southern Illinois and Southern Missouri. It didn't kill very many people — maybe a couple here or there — so it didn't really make the national news. I never heard about it, and Alejandra said she never heard about it either because she was still up in Chicago. Then again, she was only 8 at the time, so I doubt she paid much attention to the news.

There's still a debate about what we should call the storm. It's officially called a "super derecho", but they had to make up that term because it was a new type of storm. People around here call it an "inland hurricane" because they say it acted like a hurricane. Whatever it was, it shut down most of the region. There was no power for days or weeks, trees in the roads, storm damage everywhere, people stranded in their homes, and so on. It was so bad that they declared some counties a disaster area.

I've seen the pics. Carbondale is the biggest town within about two hours of here and it was shut down. It was worse in some of the smaller towns and rural areas. Trees everywhere, some buildings smashed, whole metal roofs just tossed in the air and tangled up in power lines. Disaster.

What's so important about this storm? Jess says that it was the first time global warming seemed real to a lot of people around here. Yes, there had been plenty of storms and tornadoes before. And yes, they had heard of global warming before. But here was this really strange storm, like nothing anyone around here could remember, and it shut whole counties down for days if not weeks. It sounds like a crazy time.

When Jess told me this story, she got all excited. She was just a little kid at the time, but she remembered exactly where she was, what she was doing, what it was like in the days after the storm, that type of thing. And at first, I just enjoyed the story because it was Jess, and she loved telling it, and I loved listening to her. But then the more I thought about it, the more I realized that it was a big deal. Something clicked, and I really understood why it was so important to Jess for me to hear this story.

How many other people have stories like this?

When people talk about global warming and storms, we tend to talk about a few of the really big storms that hit really big populations — Hurricane Katrina, Hurricane Sandy, Typhoon Haiyan, Typhoon Usagi, Hurricane Rafael, and now Hurricane Florence. They do seem to be getting worse, especially now that the sea level is higher and a storm surge that used to be no big deal can flood an entire city.

But what about the May 8 inland hurricane? What about some nameless wildfire that swept through some town out West and changed the lives of a few thousand people? What about some drought in the Middle East that doesn't seem to kill anybody but leads to another war a few years later? What about some flood in China that I never even heard about but caused a landslide and brought destruction to a city there that will be remembered for generations?

There must be so many moments like this with global warming — moments that never make it on the news or get written down in history books because the city wasn't big enough, or not enough people died, or it was too far away, or you can't be sure it was just global warming. But these things are happening. And they're changing people's lives. They may not understand it at first, and they may not believe it at first. But give them time and they will understand. They will believe.

And they will act.

I don't have all the answers. I'm just someone who grew up in Miami and wants to go back home. But this weekend, everyone who has been touched by global warming can meet up and figure out what to do together. When I think about how many people have been touched by this — directly, personally — part of me feels scared. This is something very big, very powerful, very dangerous that has been brought on us by human action. But another part of me feels oddly comforted. Because whoever you are, wherever you live, this has touched your life. You are not alone here, and you don't have to be alone as you struggle to find solutions that work for you and your people.

This is a tough time, but we're all in this together. And together, we can make a difference.

GLOBAL CONFERENCE ON MIAMI
August 2, 2030 at 13:16

¡Dios mío! What a crazy day! So much has happened and I'm so exhausted that I don't even know where to start. I guess I'll start at the beginning.

When I woke up this morning, I thought everything was fine. I woke up early so that I could borrow Alejandra's car and drive to campus for some last minute preparations for the Global Conference On Miami, which is the name we eventually settled on for all of the local Miami Meetups and Miami Ally events. So I woke up, took a quick shower, got dressed, ate a quick breakfast, and headed out the door.

When I went outside, I found out that Alejandra's car had been attacked.

I say attacked because of the amount of damage. The tires were slashed, the windshield was smashed, and the headlights and tail lights were all broken. There were even some dents and scratches in the body. Honestly, I'm surprised we didn't hear it happen. The parking lot isn't right by our door, but we can see it from the window. They must have done it while we were listening to music or watching a movie. Maybe they even had someone watching us through the window to see if we would call the police. That's creepy. I feel like one of the neighbors must have seen it, but either they didn't call the police or the police didn't care.

I feel so bad about Alejandra's car. I doubt her insurance will even cover it all. I know it's not really my fault, but it feels like it. She tries to avoid being political, and I did too before Florence. We didn't want any trouble. We just wanted to live our lives, go to our jobs, mind our own business, hope for the best. But when you see your whole city go underwater, it changes you. I like the way Jess puts it. You can't be neutral on a moving train. Saying nothing, doing nothing, that's political too. So I have to do something.

Anyway, there I was, staring at a car that had been smashed to pieces. Once the shock wore off, I realized that I was going to be late. I ran inside, told Alejandra, and ran out to the bus stop. I missed the bus, so I had to walk to campus. I got there almost an hour late.

The campus was in a state of chaos. The newly formed Constitutional Militia Coalition of Southern Illinois had deployed hundreds of people to intimidate greens and try to keep them off campus. There are a few entrances to campus, but the main one is a three-way intersection that has two corners on campus and a long parking lot and woods across from campus. About a hundred of the CMC troops were standing on those two corners in camo uniforms, many of them wearing body armor and helmets in spite of the summer heat. They carried no weapons, though, because they were choosing to respect the university's gun restrictions, at least for today. Instead, they carried these big American flags and printed signs saying that the global warming is a hoax, Green Front should be arrested, shut down the conference, those types of slogans.

Across the street, there were dozens of men and a few women in similar gear who were all carrying assault rifles. They weren't pointing them at anyone, but something about the way they were carrying them was scary. They weren't just there for appearances. They were all on edge, keeping an eye on passing cars, the edge of the woods, and so on. They weren't aggressive, but they were ready to shoot people if they needed to.

And that was just the CMC! There were two foot bridges nearby that go over the main street. Both of those had been taken over by men in black body armor with assault rifles. I didn't see any badges, but since they had guns on campus, my guess is Homeland Security, or maybe some Bastion men who had been deputized. There were also some military vehicles driving on and off campus slowly, staying mobile but keeping an eye on the situation.

There were a few dozen Green Guard there too. They were all standing on the side with guns, at least the ones that I could see. They were easy to distinguish because of their bright green helmets and a banner that simply said "MIAMI". The CMC taunted them by shouting insults and threats, but the Green Guard were very disciplined, talking among themselves but not getting drawn into a shouting match. I was surprised, actually, because a lot of Green Front people who aren't in the Guard seem to take great pleasure in shouting back and making a scene.

The CMC troops were definitely intimidating. They did their job well. I had to walk past them to get on campus. I suppose I could have turned around and found another way, but I was already late, and I didn't want to give them the satisfaction. So I walked past them. They shouted all sorts of things at me about how global warming was a hoax and I was a fascist and a terrorist and a traitor for attending the conference. At one point, someone shouted "That's her! That's the one!", and then everyone got twice as loud and excited with all of the insults. They kept their hands off me, though, so I guess that's something.

When I made it inside the student center where they were having the first big event, I felt much safer. There were still some unarmed CMC troops there, but it was quieter, and there were hundreds of green people who were there for the conference. It hadn't officially started yet, but they were all checking in and talking to each other outside of the ballrooms while they waited for it to start.

I was so relieved when I saw Jess behind one of the registration tables. She was having an animate conversation on the phone with one of the other organizers. I hurried over to her and she took a break from her call to give me a big long hug. Then she pointed at a to do list on her tablet and we started working.

Most of the events inside the conference have gone really well so far. The turnout is better than we expected, which has created some problems, but it also means more volunteers. So when the food runs out, we have plenty of people to go make a run into town for more. And the telepresence technology that Ermete and his team set up was absolutely beautiful. I'll talk more about that next time, but I have to at least mention it now. The global keynote speakers were broadcasting from Miami. They set it up so that every local event felt like they were in the front row seats. But then you could look at the walls to your left, your right, behind you, and see all of the people from all of the events in other cities. It's amazing what you can do with a few good projectors, some cameras, and some decent bandwidth. I was in a big ballroom with just a few hundred people, the same room that the panel discussion happened in. But I felt like I was surrounded by everyone in the world who was attending their local Conference on Miami. It was amazing.

The smaller workshops and discussions were great too. It's the same basic idea as the ballrooms, but smaller and more interactive. I went to a discussion about green solutions for some of the infrastructure problems Miami is facing. Some of it was specific to Miami but some of it could apply to other cities. There were four cities involved in this meeting and each city had about a dozen participants. The telepresence technology made it feel like we were all in a single oddly-shaped room having this conversation. Some of us even talked informally afterward like you would at an in-person conference. I may have a good lead on a project in Miami that's looking for new volunteers and staff.

The only down side during the conference itself was that one of the meetings was disrupted by infiltrators. They registered for the conference, attended a few events, and then suddenly just started ranting and screaming and attacking one of the telepresence projectors. I wasn't there for it, but I'm pretty sure I heard it down the hall. They didn't have guns, thank God, but they were escorted out of the building by a few of our unarmed security volunteers.

I just want to go on and on, but I need to try to get some sleep. I have to be up again in a few hours so that I can help with a few things in the morning before the next event. A few of us are sleeping on the couch and floor at Gaia House tonight so that we won't have to walk or drive home between now and then. Ermete is sound asleep in a sleeping bag on the floor right next to me. His tablet is still in his hand and he's using his bag as a pillow. Jess is sitting by my feet at the other end of the couch. She's staring at a screen and typing. I wouldn't be surprised if she's posting somewhere about her experiences today too.

It's been a crazy day, but so far, so good. I'll try to post again tomorrow. If I can't find the time, I'll let you know how it went when it ends on Sunday. Wish me luck. And if you're not at local conference already, you still have time to get there. Trust me, it's worth it.

GCOM DAY TWO
August 4, 2030 at 21:39

Yesterday was the second day of the Global Conference On Miami. I tried to post about it last night, but I was so tired and sore and emotional that it just wasn't coming together. Ermete saw me struggling with it and convinced me to just save my progress as a draft and finish the rest tomorrow.

Ermete is a wise man.

I spent Friday night sleeping on the couch at Gaia House. I tried to just sleep on the floor and offer the couch to other people, but they all insisted I should have the best spot. Jess joked that I was getting special treatment because I was a Miami refugee, but really, that's just how they are. They seem like the type of people who would give the shirt off their back to someone in need. This town is still strange to me, but they make me feel at home.

The second day also seemed to start smoothly at first. Sometimes I wonder if the anti-greens just like lulling me into a false sense of security. I woke up, ate a quick breakfast, had a good talk with Jess, and headed over to campus. The crosswalk between Gaia House and campus is a block or two away from that big main entrance, so I was able to avoid the worst of the denialist sideshow for a little while. But the Constitutional Militia Coalition obviously knows that Gaia House is involved in the conference, so they had about forty unarmed troops right by the crosswalk. They're willing to wake up pretty early in the morning to harass some greens, I'll give them that much.

Once I got past the loudmouth bullies on the corner, everything seemed great. I helped set up the main information table for the morning, ran a few errands on campus, and got everything done in time to check out one of the morning's first workshops. I was in one of the ballrooms upstairs with maybe 75 other people. We had just gathered into smaller circles with each group discussing some aspect of global warming solutions for large cities.

And then the power went out.

You have to understand that three of the four main ballrooms in the student center don't have any windows. That's where most of us were during the morning workshops. So when I say that the power went out, what I mean is that a few hundred people spread out over three or four large rooms suddenly found themselves in near darkness. There was some emergency lighting, thank God, otherwise it would have been total darkness.

There was a moment of panic. And then the workshop leader urged everyone to remain calm and reminded us that this was one of the situations we knew to expect. We just had to remain calm and proceed to the exit in an orderly fashion.

And then came the teargas.

Somebody in the ballroom opened up a can of teargas and threw it into the center of the room. I didn't see it happen, but they must have been sitting by the door, because that's where it came from. By the time I turned around, he was already slipping out the door and shoving it shut behind himself.

Everybody started to panic. It wasn't as bad as it could have been, of course. It wasn't wild panic, just a rush to figure out what to do before the gas got too bad. We all knew something like this might happen, and we all figured out pretty quickly what the guy's plan was. Open some teargas, lock the door, let us choke for a while.

What really helped save the day was the Green Guard.

I didn't mention this here, but a few days ago, I got a call from someone in the Green Guard. He was a local, so at first the local number and southern accent made me think it was another bad phone call. But he was very polite and friendly and told me that the Green Guard wanted to help with security for the conference. Half of them would serve as armed guards out on the street in case the CMC flipped out and started shooting people. But the other half would go undercover, attending the conference like anyone else but quietly making sure that each meeting space was protected.

I really wanted to talk about this secret plan on here. Green militias? Undercover security guards? I've never been involved in anything like this before. It was all exciting and a little bit scary. But obviously I couldn't talk about it until after the fact. It would have spoiled the surprise.

The element of surprise came in handy. It sounds like the people who did this weren't expecting so much resistance. They planned to just throw the teargas, slip out, chain the door, and run outside to blend back into the crowd. One of them managed to get the chain on, but the other three didn't even get that far. They were tackled by undercover Green Guard and held on citizen's arrest until the police arrived. The one who was quick with the chain did manage to escape. But we got some video, so hopefully they'll catch him.

And then there was the power guy. There was one guy whose job it was to shut down power in the building at just the right time. He almost got away because it was dark and Green Guard only had two guys nearby. But then some bystanders saw him running from Green Guard and figured out that he was the guy who had shut off the power. There was a brief fight but nobody was seriously hurt.

That's the theme for all of this chaos. No one was seriously hurt, thank God. Someone could have been trampled, or someone with asthma could have breathed the gas and died, or who knows what else could have happened. But most of us got out of the room in time to avoid the full effects. The people chained inside that one ballroom had it the worst. A few people did have to get checked out by paramedics for breathing problems or minor injuries they sustained during the chaos. The rest of us just had to wash our eyes and our skin with the help of first aid volunteers. I tripped and fell on someone's backpack in the dark, but luckily I didn't break anything. I don't think I even sprained anything, although my left shoulder is still a little sore. Annoying but no big deal.

That was the biggest disruption of the day on Saturday. Of course, we didn't let it get to us. A few people decided they were done for the day, but most of us stuck with it. We went outside into the heat, gathered in a field and parking lot nearby, and continued our discussion. The conference ran late for the rest of the day, and we didn't do as much of the telepresence work as we planned because some of that was supposed to happen in the ballrooms. And we got harassed repeatedly by unarmed CMC troops, random protesters, and even a few of the armed Bastion troops, which was a little scary. But then some Homeland Security people in suits told Bastion to pull back, and they did.

All things considered, we made a good recovery. The conference resumed and we made it through all of the programs we had planned. It was a very stressful day, but also a good day. It was all worth it.

Today was also exciting, but mostly for other reasons. I'll post about that tomorrow. In the meantime, this seems like a good stopping point. Thank you to everyone around the world who participated in your own local session of the Global Conference On Miami. Some of you had it worse than we did, but as far as I know, all of us in over four hundred cities kept it together in some form for a full day of events. That's quite an achievement.

GCOM DAY THREE
August 5, 2030 at 23:16

What a weekend! I still haven't explained what happened on Sunday. It's hard to put into words, but I'll do my best.

Out of all three days of the conference, Sunday was the one with the least problems. Saturday was the most stressful and probably the most exciting because we got attacked with teargas and had to struggle just to keep the conference going. It was hard, and some people were driven away by fear and injuries, but there was also a sense of triumph because we didn't let the denialists shut us down. On Sunday, there wasn't quite the same adrenaline rush, but it may have been the most satisfying. There were still some problems, but we knew it was nothing we couldn't handle. We just went ahead with our schedule and had a strong finish.

The morning started early with a few different Sunday worship services, including Sunday mass for Catholics. The theme, of course, was global warming and social justice. I should have mentioned last time that on Friday and Saturday, there were other services for people of other religions and beliefs, including one for the atheists and agnostics. But I got so caught up in the chaos on Saturday that I didn't say much about the full schedule of events. Anyway, after all of the worship services, there was also a big interfaith service lead by the Carbondale Interfaith Council where people of all religions and beliefs came together to express their shared moral concern about the climate crisis and hope for the future. Each person spoke or sang or prayed for just a couple of minutes because there were so many people to get through. I had never even heard of some of those religions before, so I may need to educate myself.

I usually only go to mass on Christmas and Easter and whenever I'm visiting relatives. I know, I should go more, but I get busy. You know how it is. Anyway, it was exciting to go and hear about the importance of taking action on global warming. I usually think of church and my green work as separate. But the Pope is all in favor of taking action on global warming, so it all makes sense. It was good to hear about it from that perspective.

The CMC and other anti-green protesters didn't try to disrupt the Sunday services. I don't know if it's because they tend to be very religious, or they didn't want to be perceived as anti-religion, or some other reason. Who knows. But they kept their distance. As soon as the religious time was over, though, they stepped up their game again, with all of the unarmed troops shifting from their spot on the edge of campus to ongoing marches around the buildings where we met. It was sometimes noisy and obnoxious, but there were no more serious attacks.

So we just had to finish the conference. There were a few smaller workshops left to do, but the two biggest tasks for the final day of the conference were the local declaration and the global virtual march and rally.

Each of the local GCOM events was asked to come up with a declaration about the Resilience Program and the Resistance Program. Some of us in Miami Diaspora came up with a sample declaration before the conference, but it was a little rough because we only had a couple of weeks to work on it. Also, each city needed to customize it a little to fit their circumstances. So by Sunday afternoon, we had worked together to come up with a local declaration to send to the media, the local city council, the state assembly of Illinois, and the federal government. To make a long story short, it said that we the people have declared that our governments and industries must take real action on these issues. If they don't, we'll do as much as we can on our own and use protests and elections to force governments and industries take action.

At the very end, it was time for the global telepresence march and rally. Each local event had a few aerial video drones so that all of us could be combined digitally into a single huge march and rally. Our local event had about a thousand people if you count the ones who just came for the rally. People are still debating the exact global turnout, but the lowest serious estimates say that it was twelve million people in over five hundred cities. Some say it was even more. It was definitely the biggest global climate march in history, especially if you count all the little actions of people who couldn't travel to the GCOM events.

The global video looked strange due to the fact that each event had different lighting, different size crowds, different architecture, and so on. But that's part of what's so interesting about it. They blended it all together as well as they could to make it look like a single global march. Millions of people from all around the world were marching together as one, calling on government and industry to take serious and immediate action on global warming. While we were marching, I didn't even bother watching most of it online because I was right there in the middle of it. But when I watched the whole thing online later, it was beautiful. You could zoom in on different parts of the march and watch people marching through cities from around the world. I don't know much about architecture, but it seems like every type was represented somewhere — skyscrapers, suburban sprawl, farm houses, beaches, hospitals, art museums, cathedrals, mosques, even some ancient monuments like Stonehenge and the Pyramid of the Sun. And people were wearing everything you can imagine, from people in the tropics running around nearly naked to people in the far north walking around in big puffy coats and fuzzy hats. It was like nothing I'd ever seen before. It was amazing.

So that was the last big event of the Global Conference On Miami. I can't speak for people in other places because some of them had it worse than we did — violent anti-green protesters, government crackdowns, and so on. But as far as I'm concerned, it was definitely worth all the trouble. It definitely made almost everyone I've talked to feel about ten times more motivated and ten times more clear on what we should do next. It also demonstrated just how many of us want to do something about global warming that will solve the problem once and for all. Now all that's left is to go back into our everyday lives with this knowledge and this motivation so that we can do the hard work that lies ahead of us.

PROSPECTS
August 8, 2030 at 22:01

After all of the excitement of the Global Conference On Miami, the last few days have seemed calm by comparison. I haven't been spending as much time with Alejandra lately, so the two of us had dinner and drinks together. It was good to sit down with her and talk all about the crazy weekend. Sometimes she's the talkative one, but she's also a very good listener when I need someone to talk to. I really appreciate that.

It's going to take some time to figure out how much of an impact the conference had. I'm sure that seeing millions of people around the world marching for the climate has made some of the politicians and business leaders take notice. Many local and national governments are also discussing specific proposals for how to take action on the climate crisis in their city. It will take time for the wheels of bureaucracy to turn and any actual changes to come through. The fact that elections are coming up here in the U.S. is a big factor. We have to wait two years for the next presidential election, but anyone in Congress who tends to oppose climate action must be sweating bullets right now. As the coasts are eroding, so is the support for denialist politicians. Their money can only keep them in power for so long if everybody insists on some serious action in response to global warming.

Big changes are on the way. In the meantime, there are plenty of smaller things to do around here. Gaia House, Southern Illinois 350,

Illinois South Solutions Project, Shawnee Green Party, Shawnee Group Sierra Club, and a lot of other local groups are working together on plans and projects related to global warming in general and Miami in particular. In fact, that brings me to the main thing I wanted to talk to today.

I'm trying not to get my hopes up about this until the details are settled. But during GCOM, I talked to a lot Miamians. Some are in the city now and others plan on going back soon. It's still rough there, but it's reached the point where they've figured out some decent and fairly reliable solutions for the necessities of life: electricity, food, shelter, even running water in some places, although that may just involve collecting rainwater. The old systems for delivering these things are mostly gone, but people are coming up with creative solutions. There's still a lot of debate about this, but some of us think it's time to go back to Miami.

I was feeling very torn about this. More than anything, I want to go back and help with the recovery. But I haven't had enough time to save up much money. The trip out there alone would eat up most of my savings. Then I would have to be sure to have some way to survive out there, otherwise I could end up stranded in the city somewhere or herded into the refugee camps. Even with the improvements, the city is still considered a disaster area and the government is actively discouraging anyone from returning unless they are directly involved in relief and rebuilding. And it would be hard to leave Alejandra and Jess and Ermete behind so soon after such an amazing weekend.

So before GCOM, and even on the first day, it didn't look good. I thought it would be months until I made it back to Miami. But then I heard about two groups of people who may be able to help me make that happen much sooner.

The first group was local. On the second day of the conference, we found out that a few local donors were willing to fund a special project to send a few people from Southern Illinois to Miami to promote socially just and ecologically sustainable solutions. This is a pretty amazing offer given what the economy around here is like. Most people simply don't have the money to spare. But there are some people here who quietly support green projects by making donations and sharing their advice and vision with the organizers. Jess tells me that they usually focus exclusively on Southern Illinois. But in this case, they're making an exception because of the situation in Miami.

There are some crazy people out on the streets of Miami right now — gangs, shady businessmen, mysterious outsiders, well-meaning but totally inexperienced entrepreneurs — who are basically just grabbing up property through a mix of legal and non-legal means. With just a few thousand dollars, or a few boats and guns, you can get your hands on buildings that would have cost millions just a couple of months ago. The remaining police force is so strapped for cash and personnel that they mostly just patrol the city and make sure that nobody's getting blatantly murdered, abducted, mugged, and so on. The people from Bastion are supposedly there to help, but they're just mercenaries. What do they care? As long as they get paid, they don't care much about the details. And it's not entirely clear who's paying them anyway. They're supposedly deputized, so the government must be involved in some way. But there may be private funding too. If there is, who knows what their goals are.

Anyway, the local donors here in Southern Illinois see the potential for major green projects to get started while the situation is in flux. It's a risky idea, but they say it's worth the risk because of what stands to be gained. What if a major American city could be rebuilt from the ground up as an example of urban ecological design? They have some very good ideas for projects in Miami, and they want to send some people from Southern Illinois to get these projects started. If it works out, these people will learn important skills, gain important contacts, and maybe even bring some money back to Southern Illinois. But they need at least some people who are currently in Miami to help get it all started.

That's where the second group comes in. Some of my contacts in Miami Diaspora are trying to start green projects but they need outside support. In theory, it's a perfect match. But it's going to take a couple of weeks to figure out the details. There are several possibilities for projects that would meet everyone's goals and visions. I can't talk about it in too much detail yet because we're still figuring it all out and the people involved don't want to go public until we settle on the details. But I've introduced a few of these people to each other online and it seems to be working out well.

I'll post more information as soon as I can. In the meantime, it's good to know that my prospects for making it back to Miami have just improved dramatically.

CONVERSATIONS AND DECISIONS
August 11, 2030 at 15:05

The past few days have been filled with important conversations and decisions. Some have happened online, some on the phone, some here at Alejandra's place, some on campus or in town. We're still working out the details, but one thing is clear.

I'm going back to Miami.

The Integral Ecology Initiative is coordinating the effort to send a team from Southern Illinois to Miami. There are many local groups supporting the effort, including those donors that I mentioned. We'll be sending a group of about fifteen to twenty people with specialized skills related to the work we'll be doing out there. My three main qualifications are my familiarity with Miami, my recent organizing work with Miami Diaspora, and my experience with photovoltaic installation.

Now that we've definitely decided to do this, the two biggest decisions are who's going and what we plan to do when we get there.

First, I want to talk about the what. I can't go into too much detail because like I said earlier, we don't want other people to take our ideas. We have a few plans finalized, a few plans in the works, and a willingness to entertain other ideas. The basic overview is that we want to experiment with various solutions to the many problems facing Miami now that most of the city is underwater. If our experiments are successful, we'll be doing our small part to turn Miami into a demonstration of green solutions to inundation caused by global warming. Ironically enough, we may also be able to take some of the lessons we learn in Miami and bring them back to other cities that haven't gone underwater. For example, learning more ways to conserve water and energy is a useful lesson in any city.

If you have any ideas, please share them in the comments or send me an email using my contact form. I prefer to communicate in the comments here on the blog because I want to create some dialog about Miami and global warming and all things related. But I do accept private messages too.

So that's the what. Now, let's talk about the who.

I'm definitely going. I've known since the moment that I started walking out of Miami that I wanted to come back as soon as possible. It's funny how sometimes you don't really appreciate something until it's gone. I've always known that I liked Miami, but you know how it is. You complain about the weather, the traffic, the crime, the politicians, and so on. But then when you have to go, you get homesick. That's how it is for me, anyway. I love Miami.

The big question is who else is going. There are already about a dozen other people who are definitely going. Others are still considering it. Keep in mind that this is a big commitment of time and energy for little or no pay. It's also a trip into a potentially dangerous situation. Lots of people want to go because they care about global warming, or they want to help Miami, but not everyone is sure they can do it. Two of the biggest question marks in my mind are Jess and Ermete.

Ermete sounds confident about going. He says he needs to see if he can find other people to pick up some of his work here in Southern Illinois. He's a genius with all things electrical and he would leave a big gap in the clean energy and information technology communities here if he went to Miami. But he also says he's a traveler at heart. He's spent most of the past year or two here in Southern Illinois. That's a long time for someone who likes to travel. It's time for his next adventure.

Jess, on the other hand, is feeling very conflicted. She and Ermete and I have become inseparable over the past couple of months, so it's hard to imagine us going our separate ways. But it's also hard for Jess to imagine leaving Southern Illinois for months if not longer. She grew up around here, and after some time out of state, she came back here because she loves the place. But one of her greatest passions nowadays is taking action on the climate crisis. She says this project is a big opportunity to get people thinking about Resilience and Resistance. But she also worries that the fossil fuel companies may make another attempt to invade Southern Illinois while she's gone. Local people have fought very hard and bitter battles to keep that dirty coal and oil and gas in the ground. They've had some victories, but there's always the risk that the companies could try again. Of course, she could always come back if that happened. So maybe she can go to Miami for a while and come back later in case of emergency.

I really feel close to Jess. When I came here, I didn't realize it at first, but I was anxious and depressed about leaving Miami and the difficult experiences I had in my last days there. Alejandra gave me a safe haven and some much-needed comfort, but it was Jess who helped me snap out of it by getting me active and involved in all of this community work. She says I helped her to get active again too because showing me around gave her a renewed sense of enthusiasm and hope. That was good to hear.

I really hope Jess comes with us on this trip so that we can continue to spend all of this wonderful time together and support each other in our work. I've been teasing her about it and making comments to entice her down to Miami. If she doesn't come, though, I will definitely understand and support her. Southern Illinois is a beautiful place and she grew up here. It's like me and Miami. If she stays here to protect this place, I'll be proud of her, and I'll come back to visit as soon as I can.

As for Alejandra, I invited her, but she says she won't be coming. She says she likes it here in Southern Illinois and doesn't have any special skills in green technology anyway. She has a point, but I still wish she would come anyway. What will I do without mi prima? Who will go out to the restaurants and bars with me or sit with me at the end of the day to talk about everything that happened in our lives? I suppose she's making the right choice for herself, but I will still miss her. I remember missing her sometimes from Miami even before all of this started. After all that we've been through in the past couple of months, though, I'm sure we'll do a better job of staying in touch this time.

That's about all the news I have for now. There's something else I want to talk about, but it's not at all related, and it deserves its own entry. In the meantime, feel free to post comments or contact me with any ideas you have about the trip to Miami. I don't know when exactly we're leaving, but it will be soon.

AROUND THE WORLD
August 14, 2030 at 00:13

Most people who participated in the Global Conference On Miami had nothing but positive feedback for us, especially at the local level. Jess says that this is a good sign since people will complain about anything and everything at a major event. The one complaint that I heard consistently, though, was that we may have focused too much on Miami.

There's probably some truth to that. We focused on Miami because a lot of the organizers were from Miami. And honestly it's the first major U.S. city to go completely underwater because of global warming, which is a big deal. People around the world were talking about Miami, so why not turn that into a conversation about global warming? Climate activists have been doing that for decades. It just happened to be a U.S. city this time. And because Miami was the conversation starter, we named this big global warming conference after Miami. But it was about so much more than just Miami.

Now that we've had this big conference, I should at least mention what's going on in other places around the world. Other people have better information and opinions on this than I do, but here are a few things I know.

First, there are all of the places going underwater. It turns out that there are a lot of major cities on or near the water — New York, Tokyo, London, Hong Kong, Washington D.C., plenty of other places I don't even think about until I read an article about them. Some of these big cities are the most powerful economic and political centers in the world. But even with all of their money and power, they can't stop the ocean and the rain. And when they take a hit, so does the rest of the world.

Some of these cities and countries didn't take global warming seriously at first. They made a lot of money from fossil fuels and they knew it would take at least a few decades, maybe even a century or two, for sea level rise to actually claim the whole city. But they're finding out that it's not just about the sea level. It's also about the flooding, the storm surges, the sewers, the leaky roofs, the power lines, all of the little details that go along with the flooding. New York and Tokyo are perfect examples of this in my mind. They've both done these tremendous projects in the last ten or fifteen years to protect their coasts from the rising tides. Things would be so much worse if they hadn't worked on these incredible systems of storm walls, berms, dikes, levees, improved sewers, and so on. But even with the ocean held at arm's length, they still get more flooding than they used to. The ocean hasn't claimed them, but they're slipping into a downward spiral. A big storm hits, they get hopelessly flooded for a while, they drain the water eventually, and then before you know it, the next storm hits. Unless you put an umbrella over the whole city, there's not much you can do about that.

And then there are the droughts! ¡Dios mío! I complained about chocolate a while ago, but in an emergency, I can live without chocolate. What I can't live without is food. Do you remember when California used to grow so much produce that they could ship it around the world? Now they can barely supply produce to other states. Food costs about three or four times more than it did when I was a kid, especially fresh produce that's out of season. Some of that is the economy making everything more expensive, but some of it is just the food being more scarce. In a lot of places, more people are buying local food now because of the price, even if they don't care about the environment or the local economy. It's just cheaper to grow veggies in a local field or greenhouse than to fight with millions of other Americans for some tomatoes and grapes from California. But then what do you do if your local farmers have a drought too?

Honestly, I know the most about what's going on here in the U.S., not what's going on in other countries. You hear about the big things, like the Maldives and Bangladesh going underwater, or the wars in the Middle East and Eastern Europe and Africa because of droughts and famines and fighting over fossil fuels and water, or the super typhoon that just hit the Philippines and may leave Manila in a worse situation than Miami. I could try to explain it all in more detail, but you can just do a search and look at the current news and the projections for the future.

If you're going to look at it all at once, though, you may want to have a few mojitos and a shoulder to cry on.

Anyway, one of the main reasons I wanted to talk about this today is to say that I'm always interested in hearing more about how people in other parts of the world are coping with global warming. People from around the world have been so kind to reach out to the Miami refugees and ask them what they can do to help. I want to do the same thing and help people in Manila, and the Maldives, and Bangladesh, and anyplace else where people are suffering from global warming. Global warming is hardest on people who are already poor, already refugees, already struggling to find food and shelter and a better life. What happened in Miami pales in comparison. And that's saying a lot since I watched my entire city go underwater! We live in strange times. Now more than ever, we need to come together to help each other.

Please feel free to post comments about what's going on where you are. I will do my best to reply and see if there's anything I can do to help. In the meantime, the struggle continues to figure out what we can do to help Miami and reduce our country's contributions to global warming.

THE RAID
August 16, 2030 at 20:54

I was picking cucumbers in the garden when the soldiers came.

It was Thursday morning at about 9:30 a.m. I'd come to Gaia House because I was feeling restless and wanted to pick some cucumbers and tomatoes before the insane summer swelter set in for the day. The college students are about to start their semester next week, so it was a busier day than it has been lately. There were cars on the street, people walking by, a group at Gaia House for breakfast and conversation, and so on. But really, it just seemed like a normal day.

There were about a dozen of us at Gaia House that morning, but only two of us were outside. I was near the back door picking cucumbers. Dharani was near the edge of the yard tending the compost pile. She's on the garden committee, so I often see her out there doing this or that when I come to Gaia House.

At first, I didn't even notice the military-style vehicles. My back was to the parking lot north of the garden and there was a hill between me and the street south of the garden. So at first, I didn't even see that about a half dozen armored personnel carriers had shown up in the parking lot and on the front lawn. Something didn't feel right, though, so I looked over to Dharani and saw a look of shock on her face. That's when I turned around to see a few dozen men in black body armor pouring out of these vehicles and rushing toward the building.

Most of the soldiers in the parking lot went straight for the back door. As I looked around in a panic, I also saw another group going in the front door. Five of the soldiers coming from the north split off from the main group and came at me and Dharani with their assault rifles pointed at our chests.

"Hands in the air! Hands in the air!"

I dropped my bucket full of cucumbers and put my hands in the air. Dharani dropped her shovel and put her hands in the air too. Each of us had two soldiers with rifles pointed at our chest. The fifth soldier had his gun held low but ready if he needed it. Keep in mind here that I'm 5'2" and about 110 pounds. Dharani is maybe 5'4" and about the same build as me, which is lean. Not that any of that should matter, but we're both so small and friendly that it's hard to imagine anyone being intimidated by us. But there they were, these huge grown men, pointing their rifles and shouting orders like we were dangerous criminals.

"On your knees! Hands behind your head!"

I knelt next to the garden and put my hands behind my head. Dharani has a bad knee, so without thinking, she put her hand on the edge of the compost bin while she was trying to kneel. The soldier didn't shoot her, thank God, but he did freak out and knock her down as if she had just reached for a weapon. Then he rolled her over on her front, knelt on her back, and cuffed her hands. I couldn't hear exactly what she was saying, but she was in pain.

After they put the cuffs on me, they searched my pockets and took my phone. Then they had me stand up and shoved me up against the wall. They made me stand there for a few minutes while they searched the building and grounds for more people.

A lot can happen in a few minutes.

The first thing was that they marched the rest of the people out of Gaia House. There were nine or ten people, all of them in handcuffs except for this one little boy, maybe ten or eleven. Seeing that boy walk out of there was such a sad moment for me. Something about the look on his face just shook me. He was a little scared, but mostly he was just sad. He shook his head and sighed, a knowing sigh that should never have to come out of the mouth of a child. They didn't cuff him, but they pointed a gun at him and made him stand against the wall with the rest of us until social services could come and get him. At least I hope they took him to social services. He was only a boy.

The other thing was scary and creepy. Once they caught everyone, a few men in suits and ties got out of an unmarked car and started talking to the men in body armor. One of the suit men walked right up to me and glared at me, glancing over his shoulder to see if his buddies were looking. When he saw that the other men were busy, he pulled out a handgun and pressed the muzzle hard against my forehead. Then he leaned in closer and whispered in my ear.

"Go home. This is your final warning."

And then he punched me! I have never felt such pain in my entire life.

He gave me a quick punch under the ribs and I just crumpled in pain. I couldn't breathe for a minute and I almost passed out. I thought I was going to be sick. I've been slapped and punched before by playground bullies when I was a kid, but obviously they didn't know anatomy as well as this guy. I didn't want to get back up, but while that guy was walking away, one of the soldiers started shouting at me. So once I caught my breath, I stood up straight and put my hands against the wall as best as I could.

After a few minutes, the soldiers started making a mess of the place. I could hear furniture moving and things crashing around inside the building. Outside, they were starting to bust open the wood of the raised beds and compost bin. Supposedly, they were looking for hidden weapons or who knows what else. But really, it seemed like they just wanted to smash everything. That's about all I saw, though, because then they marched us into the van.

The whole ordeal took about twenty four hours for me. After the raid, they drove us around for about twenty minutes and then locked us up in separate rooms. We arrived in an enclosed garage, so I don't even know if the place was a police station or some weird Homeland Security detention center. I spent about a dozen of those hours in a small windowless room with nothing to do. They would come in occasionally and ask me questions.

"Are you a member of the Green Front?"

"Are you a member of the Green Guard?"

"Where are your weapons?"

"Who's funding your trip to Miami? What do you plan to do when you get there?"

At some point in the week before the conference, Jess explained to me what I should do in these types of situations. I mostly just said that I wanted to talk to a lawyer. Every once in a while, they would get me to say something more, like saying I was staying with Alejandra, or saying I don't own any guns, which is true. But then I realized I should stop talking because they can trick you into saying all types of crazy things if you start talking. So I just kept asking for a lawyer.

They never let me talk to a lawyer. But they eventually put me in a slightly bigger room with a small window on the door, a little cot attached to the wall, and this weird thing that was some combination of a drinking fountain on top and a toilet on the bottom. Gross. I spent the night in that room, sleeping occasionally and wondering if they were going to send me to some secret prison for the rest of my life.

I started to lose my sense of time. There was no clock, no one to talk to, and I could barely hear anything from outside the room. It was crazy.

But then eventually, they just opened the door, put me in cuffs again, put me in the back of the van alone, and drove me to the Carbondale train station. Then they took off my cuffs, kicked me out of the van, and left.

It was all so strange and disorienting. They had taken my phone and my money, so I had no way to call anyone. Carbondale is a small town, so I decided to just walk to Gaia House and call someone from there.

It had been almost a day since the raid, but Gaia House was still a mess. The soldiers had gone out of their way to ruin most of the garden, trampling the parts on the ground and smashing open the raised beds. There were still parts that were fine, but only because they hadn't bothered to be methodical about it. When I went inside, a few people were there doing some cleaning. Not much was actually broken, but they had dumped a bunch of old paper files, emptied out some boxes, and taken every computer, phone, or other electronic device in the building. I knew it was a long shot, but I decided to go into the office in search of a phone.

And there were Alejandra, Jess, Ermete, and a few other people all standing in a circle and talking to each other.

I have never been so happy to see anyone. I ran up to them and we all hugged and cried and talked about what happened. They filled me in on some more of the details. It was a Homeland Security raid, and it was part of a big day of raids across the country. The media said it was part of a counter-terrorism effort, but a lot of people see it as payback for the conference. Everyone else in town who was arrested got released last night, so people around town were starting to believe that I was one of maybe a hundred people across the country who were being detained indefinitely as enemy combatants. They were in the office talking about who else they could contact about finding me, when they should hold a rally demanding my release, and so on. And then I walked right in the door! They were really happy to see me too.

For the moment, everything's starting to settle down. After Alejandra gave me some real food, we all spent a little while cleaning up Gaia House and talking about our next steps. Then I had dinner with Jess and Ermete. After dinner, Jess brought me to the library so I could write all of this about the raid. Posting new entries may be harder for a little while because Homeland Security took everything remotely resembling a computer. I'll just have to come here with Jess or get help from someone who's house didn't get raided.

It's good that no one was shot, and it's good that they released us all, and it's good that I can still go to Miami soon. But some of the details may have to change now. Our donors will have less money than they used to because they're helping Gaia House recover from the raid. There are also a couple of people who may just stay home now for various reasons. Jess is on the fence again about going to Miami, but I think she'll come around tomorrow after a good night's sleep. In the meantime, I should probably go home with her so we can both get some sleep. Thanks for reading all of this, and if you got raided too, let me know if there's anything I can do to help.

PREPARATIONS
August 19, 2030 at 22:34

We're moving forward with the trip to Miami. The guy who punched me in the liver and told me to go home will be happy to hear that I'm leaving as soon as possible. All that's left is to make some preparations.

There are thirteen of us going on this trip. It's not quite as big of a team as we originally planned because of the trouble at Gaia House and a few other random details that came up in people's personal lives. I guess moving away for an unspecified amount of time is a big deal for people who aren't already refugees! But it should be plenty of people for what we have in mind.

I don't really think of myself as a leader, but I've been asked by a few people, including Jess, to be the team leader. Honestly, I objected at first. My past experience with community organizing has usually just involved showing up and doing simple tasks, not being an organizer myself. But the people at the Integral Ecology Initiative said that they were impressed with my work on the Global Conference On Miami, and Jess and Ermete kept carrying on about how charming I was and how if anyone could convince people to follow her on an expedition into the lost city of Atlantis, it would be me. It was all a bit silly and over the top, but I didn't mind.

Each person on the team has special skills related to our mission of turning Miami into a model of green design. We tried to get people who each have a few different skills so we could cover our bases and have some overlap if possible. I'm the main person with contacts in Miami, and I have some technical knowledge and experience that will come in handy. Jess is finishing up her master's degree in Environmental Communication, which is the main reason IEI wanted her to come along. Some of the other supporters didn't consider that "practical enough", but Jess was quick to point out that she's also a lifelong Girl Scout with a lot of additional survivalist and First Responder training that may come in handy in a city that is still officially considered a disaster area. And Ermete is basically a genius who could be building supercomputers or warp drive for some corporation, but instead he wanders from town to town bringing the wonders of advanced technology to any local green groups that are willing to reward him with good food, good music, stimulating conversation, and some cuddling every now and then. He's such an amazing man.

The other ten people are all people I've met at some point, but I don't know them as well. Speaking of ten, one of them goes by the name Ten, short for Tenalach. She's a certified permaculture consultant who advised Gaia House on their garden design along with a couple of other permaculture people. She's also apparently a local legend, a spiritual teacher who travels every once in a while to lead workshops about how to live in harmony with the land, water, and air through an interesting combination of mystical personal practices and a science-based approach to the design of food systems and infrastructure and so on. I look forward to talking to her about that more once we're out there.

The other nine have a mix of skills related to our mission. Honestly, I don't know them as well, so I couldn't do their skills and their personalities justice from memory. But it was an impressive list of skills and an impressive group of people. We've only had one official team-wide meeting, so I'm still learning all the details. See what a good leader I am? I'm already falling behind and we haven't even left yet. I'm sure I'll have much more to share about them all once we're actually working together.

We're taking two vehicles, or three if you count the boat. Our main vehicle will be an electric bus. The bus is an old 2017 model that we were able to get dirt cheap because of its age and limited range. It was designed for small urban routes, so it was only rated for 200 miles per charge, which is probably down to about 160 at this point. Ermete says he can get it up to maybe 250 before we leave. Even so, it's going to take a few days to get to Miami, probably more like a week. On the plus side, that gives us the opportunity to make a few stops at local community centers along the way. Ten says that turning problems into opportunities is one of the principles of permaculture. Sounds good to me.

The second vehicle is an electric van. I don't know too much about it, but it's green and it looked like it was in good shape. The back is already loaded up with extra batteries to extend the range, which is especially important since it will be towing the boat. I don't know much about boats, but it's a little speedboat that will supplement the larger boat (or boats?) provided by our partners out in Miami.

So when are we going to leave? That's a good question. It could be as early as next week. I've asked everyone to be ready to leave next Monday, and then we can just stick around another week or so if we have to. But it will definitely be sometime in the next week or two.

I have such strange mixed feelings about this whole trip. The idea of leading an expedition to Miami is both exciting and scary. Leadership of any type is still new to me, and the road to Miami is long, and the destination itself is still a very troubled city. The ocean did reclaim it a couple of months ago, after all. Also, I've made a lot of friends in Southern Illinois, and I'll be leaving most of them behind, including mi querida prima, Alejandra. What will I do without her? My refuge, my partner in crime, the sister I never had?

But any time I feel down about all that, I remind myself that I'm going back to Miami! This is what I've wanted all along. I know it's not the city that I grew up in anymore. There's no going back to Miami, at least not the Miami of my childhood. The bright, shining, colorful Miami that stood proudly on the shores of a swampy peninsula that was once thought uninhabitable by settlers. The Magic City that people came from all around the world to visit and live in. No, that Miami has gone the way of the dodo, the passenger pigeon, the black rhino, the mountain gorilla. But I'm looking forward to meeting the new Miami, a city already called Atlantis by some of the more melodramatic people I know, a city with a tragic past and troubled present but possibly a bright future. A future that I want to be a part of.

See, I'm already getting excited about going back to Miami. Maybe I'll be a good leader after all. In the meantime, there is so much preparation to do. I'll be sure to post any major updates as they come up. And then once we're ready to go, I'll post about our departure and our adventures on the road to Miami.

ONE LAST WEEKEND
August 23, 2030 at 12:47

There's a lot on my mind right now. Yesterday, I almost wrote an entry called "Goodbye Manila" because Super Typhoon Malakas has left the capital of the Philippines in a state of chaos. It's been almost two weeks since the storm made landfall and it still sounds like a rough situation. Hundreds of people lost their lives during the initial storm and tens of thousands more have been displaced by the damage and flooding. They're still struggling to deal with the aftermath and restore basic services to the city. It's at a higher elevation than Miami, though, so there's much more prospect for rebuilding. I decided not to write the entry because I don't want to get carried away and declare a city lost when it still has a chance of bouncing back. It's their capital after all, so they'll probably work out something to keep it going no matter what. I do have this sinking feeling, though, that at some point there's going to be a blog called Goodbye Manila, and Goodbye Tokyo, and Goodbye New York, and who knows what else.

There are a lot of other climate-related problems too — the drought in Southern Illinois and much of the Midwest, the increasing severity of the megadrought out in California, the wildfires that we often don't even fight anymore, the flooding in dozens of coastal cities. and so on. It really seems like a lot is going on right now.

And then there's everything local. Cleaning up Gaia House was quick, but replacing the stolen computers and tablets is taking time. The raised bed garden was almost a total loss and parts of the other gardens were damaged too. And now they're debating about policy. This is an all-inclusive community center where students and other community members go for all sorts of normal, peaceful social events like dinners, meetings, classes, music, worship services. Some people are saying that they need to distance themselves from any group associated with Green Front because it's too political and dangerous. But others say that they need to stick with their values and welcome all nonviolent people who want to take action on global warming and the social justice issues related to it. They're having special meetings and debating how to handle the situation. I've been attending some of it, but honestly I don't know what advice to give them since I won't be around here much longer.

That brings me to the main reason I actually sat down to write this entry. Ever since I joined up with Miami Diaspora and started working on GCOM, it feels like I've hardly spent any time with Alejandra. I technically see her every day – we live together, we sometimes have meals together, she sometimes comes to the events, and so on. But I mean real quality time con mi prima. Having a nice long dinner together. Watching some movies so we can laugh and cry together. Having drinks on the beach if we even had a beach around here. Instead we have to go to the bars and restaurants and pretend we're on the beach. That's the type of quality time I've been missing out on lately. And I'd better enjoy it while I can because it's really starting to look like I'll be leaving for Miami sometime next week.

So I've decided to spend one last weekend out with Alejandra. I talked to her about it and she really likes the idea. We haven't come up with any details yet, but I'm sure we'll find the right kinds of mischief to get into. We always do. It's also my last chance to get a good long look at Southern Illinois before I go, so we'll probably do something out on the town instead of just staying home for drinks and movies. I'm really looking forward to it, especially after how rough everything has seemed lately. It will be a good way to spend my last days in Southern Illinois.

My Last Weekend In Southern Illinois
August 26, 2030 at 21:51

I just finished up my last weekend in Southern Illinois — and it was a good one.

First, Alejandra took me to a drive-in movie theater. Yes, you read that right. A drive-in movie theater! Did you know that those still existed? They apparently still exist around here. We never went to any drive-ins when I was a kid, so I thought they were all gone. But there are still a couple dozen scattered across the country, mostly in rural areas where car culture hasn't died out yet. More than half of the cars looked like old gas-guzzlers, which was very strange. It seemed like a place from the past.

Since it was an hour and a half away, we took Alejandra's Tesla. Honestly, I would have turned her down if we were burning gas to get there. Expensive and wasteful. But it was her Tesla charged with solar power from Gaia House, so it was cheap and easy.

The drive-in was showing two movies for the price of one, so we spent about four hours out in a field watching movies and eating pizza and candy. It was great to just let go and eat junk food and watch movies for a while. The heat was intense even though it was after sunset. But there was a nice breeze sometimes, and we were in shorts and tank tops, so that helped. I miss the days when there used to be misting tents at outdoor events like that, but now water is too expensive to waste it on a misting tent.

The first movie was basically a superhero movie that took itself very seriously. It was about a woman whose family was killed in an earthquake caused by fracking, so she becomes a superhero and fights the evil corporation that killed her family. It was actually pretty good, but I wish they had cracked a few more jokes instead of playing it off as a serious action movie. You can only be so serious when your main character is wearing tight black body armor that makes her almost look naked.

The second movie was an independent film that was actually about global warming, at least in a roundabout way. It was about an environmental activist named Sarah whose life changes when she somehow stops a car crash with her mind. She realizes that something strange is happening and has to go on the run because she's being chased by a big government conspiracy. Along the way, she meets some interesting friends, has a few more strange experiences, and tries to mobilize more action on global warming. It was a little random but I liked it anyway.

We had a good time in spite of the heat. And then on Sunday, we went to the beach! It wasn't a real beach by the ocean, of course. We're hours and hours away from the ocean. But it was a big lake with a small sandy area that was about as close to a beach as you can get in Southern Illinois. It was too hot to spend all day out there, but we went swimming, laid out on blankets drinking, watched all the people out on the water, and even played beach volleyball with some of the college students. When we were kids, I used to always be better at it because I was a few years older and went to the beach more often. But Alejandra must have been practicing! We decided to switch teams at one point, and there was just no stopping her spike. She was really good.

Anyway, I don't know how exciting that is to most people, but that's how I spent my last weekend in Southern Illinois. I already did the last of my packing on Friday. Everyone else who's going with to Miami did their packing over the weekend as planned. We didn't end up leaving today, and we probably won't leave tomorrow since Jess and a couple of others won't be available until the afternoon. But we should leave by Wednesday at the latest. I'll try to post something on the day that we leave, but if not, I'll post as soon as I can. We'll be on the road for about a week, but I should have time to post as usual while we're traveling. It's a long trip to Miami, but I'm really looking forward to it. You have no idea. Wish me luck!

MEMPHIS
August 28, 2030 at 16:20

We're on the road! It was hard saying goodbye to Alejandra and some of my new friends in Southern Illinois. I still remember mi prima waving goodbye as our little caravan pulled out of the parking lot across the tracks from Gaia House. I'm sure I'll be back to visit someday, and maybe she'll visit me in Miami someday if our mission goes well. In the meantime, it helps that some of my new friends are coming with me — and our destination is Miami!

This is going to be a long trip. Instead of pushing for maximum speed, we decided to make a few stops along the way. This will give us time to recharge the bus and van at our leisure. It will also give us an opportunity to meet with other people working on global warming or Miami or anything similar. Depending on how long each stop takes, it should take us between seven and nine days.

Our first stop is Memphis. After an uneventful trip of about three or four hours, we made it here in time for lunch. I had never been to Memphis before, but it seems like a nice city. After living in Carbondale for a few months, it's good to be back in a big city again. It's not as big as Miami, of course, but there's a lot going on here. There's music, food, culture, so much more than you can fit into even a progressive small town. I've only been here for a couple of hours, so I don't really have a sense of the city yet. We'll be here until the morning though, so I may have a little time to explore later.

It's hard to compare heat at a certain point because almost everything south of Canada right now is hotter than any human being should have to put up with. But Memphis does seem hotter than Carbondale. It wasn't bad in the van, but now that we're out in the heat, I can really feel it. The heat itself is actually one of the major problems that people in Memphis have to deal with because of global warming. What was already a hot city now gets even worse during the summer, leading to all sorts of heat-related illnesses. Not to mention the way that it affects the smog, the allergens, and so on. Thank God I've got no allergies and a good set of lungs. For now, anyway.

Ermete, Jess, and I were in the van with Tenalach, the permaculturist, and Harold, one of the team members who I didn't know very well before the trip. He's a big middle-aged black man who speaks softly but firmly, loves to farm and garden, tinkers with mechanics and electronics, and knows more about survivalism and self-defense than I ever will. Even just with three or four hours on the road, the five of us have already had some interesting conversations. We come from different backgrounds, and we have different beliefs, but we're all really passionate about taking action on global warming. It's interesting to hear the different ways we each explain it, the points we agree and disagree about, and so on.

Our stop here in Memphis is simple. We're dropping off a few old laptop computers and some gardening supplies that they need for a new community garden. Memphis has a whole network of community gardens called Grow Memphis that has really helped them build their food independence over the past few decades. This is part of the Resilience program that we were talking about at GCOM. And the higher food prices get, the more people realize the value of having community gardens. So we're giving them some supplies and helping them for a few hours with some free design consultation from Tenalach and basic manual labor from the rest of us. In return, they're giving us some food and medical supplies to take with us to New Orleans. We have a small amount of room to spare on the bus, so we decided that we may as well work out little trades like this to make the most of our trip. It also helps us to ensure that we have a friendly place to park our vehicles and maybe even sleep for the night if they have room. There are thirteen of us total, though, so most places probably won't have room for most of us.

That's all I have time to write about today. We have some more volunteering to do at the garden, and then I'm going to meet up with another Miami refugee who has decided to stay in Memphis and work on global warming with a few local groups. After that, maybe I'll have time to check out the music and the bars. Who knows, I may even sleep at some point. I'll post as often as I can on the road, but as you can see, I may be busy. In the meantime, wish us luck in our travels. The farther south we go, the more conservative it gets, so we could use all the luck and prayers we can get.

JACKSON, MISSISSIPPI
August 29, 2030 at 23:17

We encountered our first delay on the way to Jackson, Mississippi. I don't know if someone told the police that we were coming or if they just saw the big green bus and couldn't resist pulling us over. But as soon as we were clear of the Memphis area, the state police pulled us over. A few more state and local police showed up within a few minutes. There was also an unmarked car which Jess insists was Homeland Security. I don't want to assume like she does, but they were wearing suits, which was strange for such hot weather.

What was the pretense? There was no pretense. I don't know what they wrote down in their paperwork, but when they talked to us, they didn't pretend that we were speeding or otherwise breaking the law. We weren't. They just asked for our papers and demanded to search our vehicles. Jess started arguing with one of the officers, insisting that he had to have "just cause" to detain us and search us. The lead officer got red in the face and shouted back at her that his "just cause" was that we were "a bunch of [blanking] Green Front [blanks] who had no business setting foot in the fine state of Mississippi." So they checked everyone's ID, checked the registration and insurance of the vehicles, searched the vehicles [including the boat], and patted all of us down thoroughly. A little too thoroughly, if you ask me.

After they searched us, they held us on the side of the road while they did some background checks and figured out if they could find any excuse to arrest us. We stood out there for about an hour in the midday heat with no shade or water while they waited on word from above. Eventually, the lead officer came back with a sour look on his face and told us that we were free to go.

All in all, it wasn't too bad. They technically violated all of our rights by detaining and searching us for no reason, but I've heard stories of worse. Crossing state lines is a lot more risky than it used to be, especially in the more conservative states. The authorities have a mistrust of outsiders and make a lot of money catching out-of-staters in speed traps, random searches, drug busts, and so on.

Anyway, once we got to our destination, it was like the difference between night and day. The climate action community in Jackson is fairly small but very happy to have out of town guests. We were greeted by an odd pair of allies — an evangelical minister who leads a faith-based global warming group and climatologist who's researching the effects of global warming on the Mississippi Delta and surrounding areas. Both of them are founding members of the Mississippi Climate Coalition. They apologized profusely for the behavior of the authorities and treated us all to a very late lunch at the minister's church.

We had planned some other activities for the afternoon, but due to the delay, we didn't have time for most of them. Jess, Harold, and I all spoke at an informal gathering of climate activists, students, faith leaders, and a few professors, while some of our other people volunteered at a local soup kitchen and food pantry. Then we had a late dinner and turned in for the night. They found actual houses for all of us to stay in! Jess, Ermete, and I are all sharing a spare bedroom in the house of an elderly woman who seems delighted to have the company. She says that she's been writing letters and signing petitions about global warming since before we were born and wishes the politicians had listened sooner.

Honestly, I wish they had too. But they didn't, so we have our work cut out for us.

On that note, I'd better get some sleep. We have a long journey ahead of us.

NEW ORLEANS, LOUISIANA
August 31, 2030 at 23:41

It's been a busy two days! After spending the night in Jackson, Mississippi, we woke up early and headed straight for New Orleans. As we drove into the city, it occurred to me that New Orleans and Miami have taken very different journeys into the ocean.

Back in 2005, Hurricane Katrina struck the Gulf Coast, leaving New Orleans and many other places underwater. Almost 2,000 people died because of Katrina and many more were displaced or otherwise had their lives disrupted. There was chaos for weeks, months, maybe even years if you count all the displaced people, the low-income neighborhoods, the city never fully repaired. The water went down in most places, but some say that the city was never really the same after Katrina. It would recover for a while, but never fully, and never for everyone.

One of the most shocking things to some people was how Bastion (which was called Blackwater back then) sent in a bunch of mercenaries with black body armor, assault rifles, black SUVs, and so on to patrol the city. That type of behavior had been going on in other countries for years, but here they were in an American city, in broad daylight, just running around harassing and even shooting American citizens with no one to answer to but themselves. That's happened a lot more since then, but it was new back then. And like most of the bad things caused by global warming, it had the worst effect on the people who were already disempowered. How much money you made, and the color of your skin, could determine whether you had your property protected by mercenaries or the mercenaries were pointing their weapons at you.

Since global warming and sea level rise takes place over the course of decades and centuries, it's hard to say when it really started becoming noticeable. But for a lot of people who weren't scientists or activists, Katrina was the first sign. So New Orleans started its journey into the ocean with a big splash. The eyes of the whole world were on New Orleans as the streets were filled with water, mercenaries, and soldiers. It made a big splash and got everyone talking about flooding, storms, sea level rise, crazy government responses to so-called natural disasters. But then for the past 25 years, the rest of it has been more of a slow creeping. There have been some terrible storms since then, especially in 2019 and 2022. But for the most part, it started very dramatically, then slowly sank into the ocean.

Miami has been the opposite. For as long as I can remember, we've known that Miami was sinking into the ocean. But it was happening so gradually that most people didn't seem to take it seriously. "Oh, we'll think of something," the politicians said. "We'll improve the sewers. We'll add some more pumps. We'll tweak the building codes. But we can't retreat from the shore. That's unthinkable."

So slowly but surely, the ocean crept into Miami. The beaches that people from around the world came to visit started washing into the sea. Flooding after storms got worse and worse. You just came to accept that certain parts of the city would be wet whenever it had rained recently. You could still drive through it, so it was no big deal, right?

And then finally, it came. The big one. Hurricane Florence. The destruction, the flooding, the storm surge so big and bad that the city would never fully be dry again.

It's different in every place. Every place has a different story, but the destination is always similar. With New Orleans, it started with a bang. In Miami, it ended with a bang. Either way, every place in the world that is on the ocean is slipping beneath the waves.

As we came into New Orleans, I felt a wave of empathy wash over me. The flooding is actually worse on the coastline around the city than it is in the heart of the city. Even so, seeing flooded areas in and around such a lively and historic city filled me with a great sadness. I felt a tightness in my chest that I haven't felt since my last day in Miami. I've watched my own city go underwater, so I could imagine what it felt like for these people, seeing that everything they had ever known was slipping beneath the waves, knowing that it was too late to stop it, stubbornly staying anyway because this was their city, the city that they grew up in, the city that they loved, and the only option for many people who had no way out.

When we arrived, we were welcomed by a large group of local community organizers. Some were local climate activists and others were social workers and social activists who dealt with different aspects of the complex challenges facing the people of "The Big Easy". They all dealt with most of the same problems, so they didn't seem to care too much if you saw yourself as a climate activist dealing with social issues or a social activist dealing with climate change. As long as you were there to help, you were welcome.

And they gave us quite a welcome! Everyone clapped and cheered and happily accepted the meager amounts of non-perishable food, electronics, medical supplies, and other supplies we had to offer. Most of that first day was spent enjoying their hospitality — the right blend of Cajun cooking, music, drinking, and dancing. Jess and I went to visit Bourbon Street, which is fortunately on high ground and has weathered many storms because of it. Ermete went to meet up with a technology collective that shared low-tech and high tech resources, including some community solar installations. Harold went to visit family and Ten went to visit a permaculture collective that was working on planting marsh grasses, trees, and other plants along the coasts to help slow down the encroaching water and wind.

The real work happened all day today. We helped distribute the food and other supplies, then we split up and worked on various projects throughout the city. Jess, Ermete, and I went to the Lower Ninth Ward, which was one of the areas hardest hit by Katrina back in 2005. For years, the area really struggled to recover, both because of the amount of damage and because they didn't really have the money to rebuild. Eventually, though, community members and allies worked together to rebuild it as a sustainable community. They have some houses with green designs, restored wetlands, and some incredible groups working on meeting people's needs and responding to the flooding and other problems. Really, what they did was turn the crisis into an opportunity to create their own new community support systems and forms of self-governance. There are still problems, of course, but it was interesting to see people working together in a variety of collectives to meet all of their needs. It gives me new ideas for what we can work on in Miami.

Ah, Miami. We will get there eventually. In the meantime, I need to sleep. It was great working side by side with these hard-working people, but it was also exhausting. We partied hard yesterday and worked hard today. Maybe that's what life is like around here. Hopefully we can bring some of that spirit with us as we get back on the road. In the meantime, sleep!

PENSACOLA, FLORIDA
September 1, 2030 at 23:55

We made it to Florida! After a few hours of mostly uneventful driving — does an "emergency bathroom break" count as eventful? — we arrived at Pensacola in time for lunch.

Pensacola's a fairly small city, but they were very welcoming, at least the people we met. We were greeted at a public event by a few members of the city's official Climate Change Task Force and some members of 350 Pensacola. Ever since the task force was formed about ten or fifteen years ago, they've helped turn Pensacola into a model of both climate mitigation and climate adaptation. All of the city's vehicles are electric and they're working on using eco-tourism and a few other green development projects to replace the revenue lost due to their eroding beaches, flood damage, and so on.

Honestly, we did less volunteering in Pensacola. After the greeting from the city, there was an informal discussion and a tour of green projects in the city. A few of us volunteered for a while at a project to rebuild and repair in an area damaged by a recent storm. Ten and Harold met up with a small group of people at a community garden and were gone for most of the day. The rest of the group just relaxed, took a day off, and maybe helped with a few odds and ends in other parts of the city.

After Jess, Ermete, and I finished our volunteering, we actually spent some time out on the beach! New Orleans isn't really a beach city, even though it's on the ocean, so this was my first real chance to spend some time enjoying the ocean.

It was wonderful! Since I've been talking so much about sea level rise, global warming, Miami, and so on, it may seem like I have a big fear or resentment of the ocean. And I will admit that at times, I do resent what human activity has done to the ocean, whether it's the rapid sea level rise, the terrifying amount of acidification, the stalling Gulf Stream, and so on. But none of that is the ocean's fault. The ocean is beautiful, powerful, liberating. When I go out in the water, or even just walk along the sand, I feel complete, at peace, at home. I can feel the ebb and flow of it even after I get out of the water. This is what's been missing from my life for the past three months.

The ocean.

After a wonderful time at the beach, we headed back to the bus and van for the night. The people in Pensacola were friendly, but not friendly enough to find us all free places to stay. So rather than waste limited funds on several hotel rooms, we decided to camp in our vehicles. It's a clear night tonight, so I'm actually sitting out in the boat and typing this beneath the stars. We're not right on the shore, but even from here, I can smell the characteristic salty scent of ocean air. It feels good.

We're in the home stretch now. Our vehicles have been providing a very good range per charge thanks to Ermete's modifications, and the fact that we're traveling in short bursts has kept us all from going stir crazy. Jess sometimes jokes about being stir crazy, but that's just because she likes to make little jokes to keep us all entertained. I thought I might get tired of it eventually, but it's actually quite endearing. It keeps us laughing. She calls all of this a big adventure — a road trip to end all road trips, a journey to the lost city of Atlantis. It's funny and the laughter helps keep us in good spirits.

I don't want to say our exact route in case anyone out there is reading this and intends to cause trouble for us. But we should be home in about two and a half more days. We'll be stopping in two more cities along the way with the third city being Miami. I'm feeling a mix of anxiety and anticipation, but mostly anticipation. Even though the Miami I grew up in has slipped beneath the waves, it will still be good to be back home.

TALLAHASSEE, FLORIDA
September 2, 2030 at 23:47

Our destination today was Tallahassee, capitol of Florida.

Honestly, I've never really spent much time in Tallahassee. I know people who went to school here, and I visited the historic capitol building on field trips, but that's about it. I also went here a few times with my mom for protests, but that was before things got worse. When I was a kid, I remember her being gone sometimes because she had been arrested. I also remember her coming home one time with a broken arm and black eye after being gone for a few weeks. She definitely didn't take me along to any protests after that.

The atmosphere in Tallahassee is so much different than it was in Pensacola. That's always been true, of course. Tallahassee is so much bigger and the politics are so different here. But Florence took all of those differences and exaggerated them. Especially all of the problems with Tallahassee.

The whole state is technically still in a special state of emergency, but it didn't feel that way at all in Pensacola. There were a few signs — more police than usual, a few armored personnel carriers tucked away in certain places, a few big unmarked vehicles that you had to wonder about. But you almost didn't notice it because it was very low-key. Our hosts were polite and friendly and didn't give us any trouble when they found out that we were staying in our vehicles rather than hotels.

Tallahassee, on the other hand, is definitely in a state of emergency. The city is full of armored personnel carriers from the National Guard, black SUVs from Bastion and Homeland Security, foot patrols by either Bastion or maybe S.W.A.T. in black body armor, and so on. It seems like martial law to me, but Jess says it's technically called a state of emergency since we have bureaucrats rather than generals running the show.

I missed out on the worst of it back in June when the first wave of refugees from South Florida made it up here. While I was making my way to Alejandra in Carbondale, some of the refugees and locals organized a massive occupation inspired by the old Occupy movement. There were thousands of people in the streets marching and rallying and pitching tents at several locations throughout the city, including the Gaines Street Commons where the original Occupy Tallahassee was located. Their demands included emergency city and state aid for the refugees so that they wouldn't end up in FEMA camps like so many others who were left homeless in the wake of Florence.

But most of it only lasted for few days. The city and state were both declared disaster areas and the demonstrators were all removed by force. The more peaceful ones were driven out, detained for a couple of days, or sent to the FEMA camps if they were homeless. But the more violent ones put up a fight — bricks, rocks, Molotov cocktails, improvised weapons, even some armed resistance. There were a few casualties on the side of government and Bastion, but about two dozen violent protesters were killed and hundreds more were arrested and charged as domestic terrorists.

After that, the streets of Tallahassee got a lot more quiet. Honestly, it's more quiet here than it used to be before Florence. You see almost as many people and vehicles on the street as you used to, but a lot of them are armed troops instead of regular pedestrians and drivers. There are still some very low-key protests and even some people camping out who have gotten special use permits with the help of local nonprofits and businesses. But it's all very subdued and a little surreal.

Of course, we were hassled when we got here. There are spots along the major routes into the city where small groups of Homeland Security and National Guard are watching the traffic. If they see anyone interesting, they pull them over.

So they pulled us over. It was the usual deal, like back in Mississippi — get out of the vehicle, give them your papers, get frisked, get your vehicle searched, get your background checked, and so on. The person leading the stop was a young woman in a suit who was much more polite than Officer Friendly back in Mississippi. But her answer was basically the same.

"All individuals and groups with any possible ties to the Green Front are automatically under suspicion of domestic terrorism. If you and your party are not currently breaking the law, or planning to break the law, you have nothing to fear."

Jess tends to be political, so she was the one really pushing the issue again this time. What about our constitutional rights? What about this amendment and that amendment? How long is this so-called "state of emergency" going to last?

The agent had a way of responding to Jess that seemed to answer all of her questions but really lead back in a circle. Honestly, I think she was just keeping us occupied while the men and women with assault rifles did the searches and ran the background checks.

After a while, they let us go. In a way, it ended up not being a big deal because they didn't detain us very long, didn't hurt us, didn't arrest us, and so on. But in a way, it's always a big deal. Our rights are eroding almost as quickly as our shores. It could be worse, but even so, it's always important to talk about it. We shouldn't just take it for granted like so many people do. Like I used to when it wasn't happening to me.

Anyway, once we made it through the checkpoint, we went straight to our destination. The local Miami Diaspora group has a small office that they use to coordinate relief efforts for displaced Miamians in Tallahassee and beyond. There was nowhere nearby to park the bus, so some of our team had to walk about a mile to get to the office. We also left two people stationed there to guard the bus.

I spent most of the day in meetings at the Miami Diaspora office. They're helping us to connect with a few other groups that also want to rebuild Miami as a model of climate mitigation and adaptation. There are a lot of people talking about some type of "green recovery" of Miami, so it's been hard to figure out who's just talking and who's actually doing anything. Today's meeting was restricted to people who are either in Miami now or people who are physically on their way there. That kept it down to a very manageable number — four of us in the Tallahassee office and two separate people joining us through some old-fashioned telepresence on two laptop computers.

While I was in those meetings, the rest of the team had their own tasks to work on. Ten and Harold went off to garden together again. I'm starting to wonder if they both just love gardening that much, or if they just like spending time with each other, or both. Whatever it is, it's good to see them working together so well. Two or three other people from our team stuck around the office for special meetings, but the rest went out to volunteer at a place nearby that served as soup kitchen and emergency shelter. Mostly it was just me, Jess, and Ermete.

Jess and Ermete spent all day and some of the night working on a project that seemed very strange but sounded like a lot of fun. It was a new crowdsourced online game about global warming. You get to play a character and respond to various situations and challenges. Ermete was mostly working on the technical end, taking a break every once in a while to sit down next to Jess and throw out some ideas about philosophy and gameplay. Jess was working with two other people on some of the ideas and systems of the game — the economics, the social aspects, little missions for the characters, and so on.

I would look over at them working sometimes while I was on break from my meetings. It was fun watching Ermete drift back and forth between jobs and seeing both of them get so excited about the details of this game. Some of it was very serious, but there was also a lot of laughing, smiling, having a good time. That was a welcome change from how stressed out and depressed we all get sometimes. They hope to work on this game in their spare time while we're in Miami. I hope they can do that too.

The game is called Adventures in Global Warming (AGW). The team that's working on it is putting a few important functions into a single game. One aspect is fundraising — having people make small donations so that their characters can buy in-game items like special clothes, a vintage Tesla Roadster, a rare speed boat, and in-game currency for other supplies, which is especially important for the characters pursuing community goals rather than getting a bunch of cool stuff. Another part of it involves education — showing people some of the current and future effects of global warming in their region. This includes making the game get harder as it goes on, which they're worried will turn off some players, but is unfortunately quite realistic. There was also some advocacy — notifications in the game about real-world actions you can take like petitioning your local politicians, buying or growing local food, and so on. It even gives you in-game rewards for donating some of your computer's processing power to various types of scientific research about global warming.

I've never really been big into online games, so it all seemed a little strange to me. Why not just do some of these things in real life instead of having your character do them in a game? But it sounds like it's going to do a lot of specific good things for the cause, not the least of which being to raise money for some nonprofits.

So that was how our day went. We're all sleeping in the office except for the guards who are on duty in shifts at the bus. Ten and Harold are both already asleep on sleeping pads. Ermete is falling asleep on a small couch. Jess is laying down on her sleeping pad and tapping on her tablet while she falls asleep. I'm sitting in an office chair because I don't like typing long entries like this when I'm fully laying down. But now that I'm done for the night, I'll go sleep with Jess and Ermete on that side of the office.

We have another early morning ahead of us. When we leave Tallahassee tomorrow, we have one more city to visit along our route. Then if all goes well, we'll be arriving in Miami the day after tomorrow. Just thinking about it fills me with a mix of excitement and apprehension that makes it hard to sleep, even as tired as I am. But I'm going to try. Wish me luck.

ORLANDO, FLORIDA
September 3, 2030 at 23:09

We got searched again on the way out of Tallahassee. Stop, check papers, frisk, search vehicles, background check, talk to Jess while she complains about the Constitution, rinse and repeat. Don't these agencies communicate with each other? Maybe they had nothing better to do at 7 a.m. Or maybe they wanted to be sure we didn't leave anyone behind to cause trouble. Either way, it didn't take long.

After our final dose of hospitality from Tallahassee authorities, we made our way to Orlando.

I'm not quite sure how to describe Orlando. The city has changed since Florence, but not in the same way as Tallahassee. Yes, there are some armored personnel carriers and occasional groups of armed troops in black body armor. But it didn't seem as severe as Tallahassee. The whole city seemed very busy and crowded, which was not too surprising since Orlando is such a tourist destination. But then it occurred to me that only the most die-hard Disney World fans would come to Orlando for tourism during a state of emergency. Most of the extra people are actually here because Orlando is just three hours away from Miami, city beneath the waves. In a way, this city has become a major "fallback point" for people running from the rising tide — or in our case, running toward it.

There are thousands of climate refugees here. Nobody knows the exact number, but it must be at least a few thousand. Since it's a few hours from Miami, they tend to be the ones who had the money and connections to get out of the city. When they came here, maybe they thought of it as an extended vacation — time to stay at a hotel and relax for a few weeks while they figured out their next steps. But then weeks turn into months, and they come to realize that they aren't as wealthy as they thought. Most of their money is tied up in a house, a car, maybe even a second car that's rusting in a few feet of seawater right now. Hotel bills add up; plans for permanent lodging fall through. Before you know it, you're camping out in your SUV, or in your thousand dollar camping gear that was gathering dust in the closet until Florence hit.

As I saw all of those people, many of them likely homeless or not too far from it, I thought about how that could have been me. If it weren't for Alejandra, I would have just drifted to a nearby city, looked for a new job, and probably ended up on the streets by now. It was a sobering thought.

We were greeted in Orlando by a newly formed coalition called Orlando Resilience and Resistance, or Orlando R&R for short. The coalition includes a broad spectrum of climate-related groups: Miami Diaspora, 350, Solutions Project, Rising Tide, a local group called Faith and Environment, and even a local chapter of the Green Guard. It also includes groups with more of a social justice or social service focus: Food Not Bombs, a few homeless shelters, a few church groups, a social service agency or two. They're all working together to respond to the many complex effects that global warming is having on the city and its people.

Our main volunteer task in Orlando was helping with the homeless situation. It was a strange mix — some of them "middle class" people who got displaced from Miami and South Florida in general; some of them locals who got displaced by rising rent and unemployment; some of them just the usual mix of people who for various reasons found themselves on the streets. Harold and a few of our team members went off with the local Green Guard to learn about the security situation in Miami and help with a new housing project. The rest of us spent all day providing food, clothing, and transportation to people in need.

It was very humbling to realize that a few more people would eat and have shelter today because we were in town — and that they may not tomorrow because we would be gone.

At the end of the day, Jess, Ermete, Ten, and I had a long conversation about the situation in Orlando and our plans when we get to Miami. We went for a long walk around a lake and sat on some benches while the sun went down somewhere beyond the trees and buildings on the horizon. The conversation was very casual, but there was often an urgency to it as one or two of us would get really excited or frustrated. There were also a few points where the conversation got so serious that we just got really quiet and thought about the situation for a while.

Ten says that we're at a strange place in a strange world.

Global warming is reaching the point where in many ways, society is starting to collapse. The economy is getting worse; people and governments are starting to panic; the ocean has claimed some outlying areas and is starting to claim major cities like Miami.

And yet we are still burning more fossil fuels as a species than we did in the 20th century.

Orlando is actually pretty good about its own emissions. There was a massive energy efficiency effort about ten or twenty years ago that reduced the carbon footprint dramatically. And since then, they've installed a tremendous amount of home, civic, and industrial PV solar systems. They're a leader in the whole Southeast region of the nation for all of that. But they are still mostly the exception rather than the rule. Even as cities sink beneath the waves, fields are scorched by drought or washed out by flood, forests are lost to unchecked wildfires, and so on, we still burn fossil fuels. It boggles the mind.

Our conversation started out as a very philosophical conversation. But then it got very practical. What are we going to do in Miami? How well is it going to work? How much of an impact will it have on the local level and the big picture?

We have some ideas, otherwise we wouldn't be coming out here. But this is all a big experiment — our trip to Miami, and humanity's trip into a climate unlike anything we've ever experienced before.

Jess is a big sci-fi and cli-fi fan, so she often talks about how she wishes she could go back in time and convince everyone to take action sooner. So much difference could have been made back in that crucial time between James Hansen's historic climate testimony in 1988 and the decades of denial and confusion that followed, all of it caused by the fossil fuel backlash.

But we can't go back in time. People were fooled for such a long time — and even when they started realizing what was going on, they didn't know what to do. They got caught up in personal fixes like buying the right light bulb, or fossil fuel schemes like fracking that actually made things worse, or feel-good protests and marches that didn't really stop the historic amounts of extraction.

So now we're left in a situation where a truly carbon neutral economy still seems so far away, yet the effects of global warming are up in our face, burning our crops and flooding our streets, making life increasingly miserable for people on the front lines while people in far away places are still making more money than they can count by burning fossil fuels.

I'm starting to sound like Jess here. She goes on a lot of rants like that. Anyway, what it all comes down to for our team is the details. We have a clear objective — go to Miami, set up a base, and build on that base in an effort to help turn Miami into a model of climate mitigation and adaptation.

Honestly, I may be ranting because I'm having trouble sleeping. This is the last night of our trip. Tomorrow, we arrive in Miami. I'm excited to be returning home; I'm curious to see how the place is doing these days; I'm excited and apprehensive about the projects we have planned and the situations we may encounter there. All in all, that leaves me more wired than a dozen cups of coffee.

But talking about it helps — talking about it with Jess and Ermete and Ten, with some of the rest of the team, with other Miami refugees, and with you, my reader. I don't hear from my readers much, but I know you're out there, and I'm always happy to hear from you and share the latest news with you. I hope that you enjoy reading these posts too. If you ever want to talk, you know where to find me.

It will take us all a few days to get settled in Miami. During that time, I have no idea how much or how often I'll post. In the meantime, keep us all in your thoughts and prayers as we take that last big step and arrive at our destination.

Next stop, Miami!

HELLO, MIAMI
September 4, 2030 at 23:58

Hello, Miami.

We arrived in Miami in the early afternoon. I don't have the time or energy right now for a full post because we've spent all day getting settled and dealing with our first set of challenges. But I wanted to post at least something here to let you know that we arrived safely.

We'll be spending the next several days establishing ourselves here in Miami. At some point, after I've caught up on sleep and work, I'll post more of an introduction to the new Miami and a description of some of our projects as they get started.

This is not the city I grew up in, but what city stays the same forever? Cities are living, breathing creatures with a life of their own. They have a certain character to them, but the details are constantly evolving. After a day of getting to know this city, I can say with some confidence that it still has enough in common with the old Miami to be worthy of the same name. No need to call it New Miami, Ocean Miami, Atlantis, or anything else. This is, in fact, Miami. It just happens to have a lot less people and a lot more water.

We have our work cut out for us, but it's good to be home.

Our Arrival In Miami
September 8, 2030 at 23:32

Hello world! After three and a half days of almost nonstop work, I'm finally ready to do some writing.

As you may have noticed, the city of Miami is more or less underwater. If you've been reading the past few entries and thinking ahead, you may be wondering what we plan to do with our bus and van. What use will they be in a city where most streets are flooded? Of course, we had a plan.

Miami Diaspora has a team of about a dozen organizers who live along the edge of the floodwaters and provide logistical support to allies living in the city. They call themselves the Liminals. The Liminals drive back and forth from a few spots of high ground north of Miami to pickup points in neighboring cities, transporting people, food, and various supplies for relief and rebuilding.

Before leaving on our trip, we made arrangements with the Liminals to donate the bus and van to them in exchange for helping us scout out a home base and giving us priority on any trips involving our old vehicles. They really needed a few large electric vehicles, and we really needed some help getting established in the city, so it was a wonderful partnership.

We arrived at a small Liminal community center in North Miami Beach just in time for lunch. After an enthusiastic greeting and a hearty lunch, we were all quick to get to work.

Now that we're in Miami, I may as well let the cat out of the bag. Harold and five of our other fellow travelers are also members of Green Guard. I didn't want to talk about this during the trip because I didn't want to draw any extra attention from the authorities or anyone else who has a problem with green militias. I also didn't want to make it seem like we were on some type of military mission to Miami. We're on a peaceful mission to turn what's left of Miami into a regional model of climate mitigation and adaptation. This involves things like solar energy, graywater systems, urban agriculture, and so on. The inclusion of members of Green Guard is simply a precaution.

As peace-loving people, we hope and pray that there won't be any violence. But let's be realistic here. Miami is mostly a lawless city at this point. There are some police left who have a serious commitment to maintaining law and order. They do what they can. But they're outnumbered by Bastion, a paramilitary security force with questionable motives and tactics. They're also outnumbered by gangs, but that's nothing new. The Florida National Guard is out on the streets in some places, but they barely match Bastion in number and have limited involvement in most of the city. Their primary mission is simply to maintain the most basic functions of government and protect what little key infrastructure is still operational. They're not here for general law enforcement purposes. And everybody knows it — including the criminals. The Florida National Guard will only interfere in local turf wars if the violence threatens to take down the entire city. Short of that, it's open season on locals and tourists who have no means of protecting themselves.

So Miami is a dangerous city right now. Bastion is running around protecting the property of wealthy absentee landowners and carving out their own little local empire in the process. Gangs are claiming territory and becoming more open in their criminality. Police are struggling to keep up — and probably getting paid or threatened into letting some things slide. Florida National Guard is just here to keep the government from collapsing — nothing less, nothing more. So by and large, the average citizen is on their own.

That's why we thought it was important to accept Green Guard's help with this mission. Of course, the people who volunteered have other skills to offer too.

Harold is a master gardener, farmer, mechanic, tinkerer, martial arts instructor, and long-time community organizer who started the Southern Illinois chapter of Green Guard a few years ago. He's also an excellent chef! Jalen is a combat medic with experience both at home and overseas. Bridget is a certified electrician and solar electric installer who also has first responder training. Murray is a plumber and sailor with a lot of experience with boats. Lou is a jack of all trades: carpenter, sailor, gardener, construction worker, martial artist, biker, musician, and more. Melissa is a botanist, herbalist, gardener, and beekeeper. They're all in their late twenties or thirties. Except for Harold, of course, who is probably in his mid-forties, although it's hard to be sure with his youthful energy. Everyone says I'm such an active person and I can barely keep up with Harold!

They all have special skills, interests, and ideas that qualify them for this mission. The fact that they also have special training and experience from Green Guard is just a bonus. It's like having a co-worker who also happens to be a Boy Scout. It comes in handy.

I didn't know any of them very well before this trip, but spending a week on the road and a few days in Miami with them has been a good opportunity to get to know them. They're all good people and we're really starting to work well together as a team.

Anyway, I've talked so much about our team and our arrival in the city that I don't have any time to get past that. I have to be up early tomorrow, so it's time to stop writing for now. I'll post more soon.

WATER, WATER, EVERY WHERE
September 10, 2030 at 22:20

I never finished talking about our arrival in Miami! A lot has happened since then, but I'll start at the beginning.

After we met up with the Liminals, it was time to explore the city and set up shop in our new home base. Since our little electric speedboat can't reasonably fit all thirteen of us in a single trip, we split into two groups. Jess, Ermete, Harold, Murray, Jalen, and I took our speedboat out for its maiden voyage while the others spent a few hours running errands with the Liminals.

The biggest challenge facing Miami right now is the water. Yes, I know, that may seem obvious. But let me explain.

The water isn't just a single problem. It's a dozen problems rolled into one. For example, as we toured the city by boat, we discovered that the depth of the water varies considerably. Most of Miami is mostly flat, but no metro area of this size is entirely flat. There's a limestone ridge that runs from about Palm Beach to just south of the city. The high ground along this ridge is bone dry in between storms, but the vast expanse of low ground all around it is now permanently underwater. And it's all connected to the ocean now, so the tides make a difference in how deep the water is, what parts of the city you can navigate by boat, what size the boats have to be, and so on. We have some ideas about new ways to deal with this, but I'll talk more about that next time.

If you took away all of the buildings, it would look like an archipelago, with the dry spots being the islands. Honestly, it might technically be an archipelago now. That's a strange thought.

As we took a look around, I talked to Jess about the tide. She's never lived by the ocean before, so the tide was just an idea to her. Here in Miami, it's always been a reality for anyone who travels by boat. Ever since Florence, that includes the majority of people left in the city.

It's strange to think that this is the only way that future generations will know Miami. Jess had never really been here before, so she will always know it as an Ocean City. Harold says that he visited family out here a few times, but never really got to know the city. Ermete is probably the only other person on our team who spent any length of time here before it sank beneath the waves. Every time we visit a new part of the city, I turn and look at him in wonder, as if to say: "Isn't this crazy? Remember what this used to look like?" He just nods knowingly, like he does sometimes when he's deep in thought.

We weren't the only boat out in the streets. Not by a long shot. There were hundreds of small craft, most of them similar in size to our speedboat. The Ocean City Resolution has broad language about boating which basically states that any seaworthy vessel that can safely navigate the city streets is free to do so. The City Commission is considering additional limits, but in the meantime, it's a free for all. There are canoes, rafts, rowboats, some larger boats here and there, and even a few small nautical drones cruising slowly but surely toward their programmed destinations.

I left Miami in the aftermath of the greatest disaster that this city has ever seen. On the day that I left, it felt like such a chaotic, dangerous, shattered place. As we toured the city by boat, though, it was exciting and refreshing to see so many people out and about on their daily business. It almost seemed normal. Some of them were commuters, like the people on the growing fleet of Green Boatbuses. Some of them looked threatening, like the big Bastion boats and the unmarked boats filled with heavily armed men in expensive clothes. Some of them were locals getting by on a small rowboat or makeshift raft. Some of them actually looked like tourists, gazing around in wonder and taking a bunch of pictures and video. Put them all together and you get something resembling a living, breathing city. It's a very different place now, but at least it feels alive again.

After taking a tour of the city and making a few quick stops along the way, we headed to our final destination: One Broadway.

Before Hurricane Florence, One Broadway was a 42 story residential skyscraper in Brickell, one of the neighborhoods in downtown Miami. I didn't know One Broadway by name, but everybody knows the neighborhood. It's the Wall Street of Miami — banks, office buildings, condos for the rich people. and so on. I never thought I would find myself living in Brickell, but here I am.

The hurricane did some damage to the building — broken windows, ground floor flooding, and a lot of other odds and ends that you don't even think about until you own a building. Under normal circumstances, this would be no big deal. It's expensive, but these things happen in Miami.

Of course, these aren't normal circumstances.

The building was without power for several weeks because the whole city is without power. Grid power in Miami has gone out entirely and won't be coming back anytime soon. The Army Corps of Engineers, the power company, and a few other big players all say that a massive construction effort could restore grid power eventually. It's feasible. But it would be incredibly expensive and nobody wants to pay for it. They also all agree that between the storm damage and the saltwater becoming a permanent part of the city, it's simply not safe to use the old lines, especially anything underground. Salt water corrodes power lines and equipment. If it hasn't given out yet, it will eventually — and it will be dangerous when it does.

That's where we come in. One of our goals here in Miami is to work on solar electric installation. Why spend countless billions on some massive city-wide engineering project when you can just replace the old system with distributed solar? The lack of grid power does create extra work, but it's still cheaper and easier than going back to the old system. The power company is sending people to City Hall and Tallahassee and even Washington D.C. every day of the week trying to convince the politicians to fund a big project to restore the grid. But considering how close Turkey Point came to a meltdown in the aftermath of Florence, why should we listen to their complaining? Thank God we were able to avoid a nuclear disaster in the middle of our hurricane disaster. I can't even imagine what that would have been like. No need to risk it again.

Of course, Miami has plenty of people who know how to install solar. But some of them – like me, now that I think about it – fled the city in the aftermath of Florence. The rest have been scrambling to meet the sudden spike in demand. Everybody wants power and most people want solar, whether it's residential or commercial. There was an anxious lull in installations right after the storm because every solar module in the city had been installed. But then a handful of companies worked on improving distribution channels. Now the installation has resumed.

We've basically come to One Broadway to set up an all-purpose workshop for climate change mitigation and adaptation. Some of that will involve solar electric installation. Some will involve creating local food systems, water systems, and transportation systems. Some of the details were planned before we came here and some are emerging now that we're here in the city. Our goal right now is to work on One Broadway itself, but our longer-term goal is to help the entire city transition in this direction. The person who ultimately owns One Broadway and other properties is actually a climate refugee himself now, so he's very open to all of this, even though it's still very new to him. He's still very business-minded about it, but he needs someone here anyway to tend to the building, and he wants to reinvent it as a green space. He really likes our idea of making Miami a model for the region. So we basically have free reign to do what we like with the building as long as we do everything we can to help the few remaining tenants and improve the value of the building.

That's about all I have time for tonight. I'll post more about our first week here soon.

Welcome To The Neighborhood
September 13, 2030 at 00:21

Moving into a new neighborhood is always interesting. It's especially interesting in a city that has recently slipped beneath the waves.

There's good news and bad news about life in Brickell. The good news is that there's almost no street crime in this neighborhood. Since the police are overwhelmed and the National Guard isn't doing law enforcement, crime has increased dramatically in some areas. Robbery, extortion, gang warfare, drug trafficking, maybe even human trafficking. There are places where even the police won't go at night. They won't admit it, of course, but make a call from that area and they won't come.

The bad news is that Bastion has a heavy presence here. The security forces downtown are a mix of National Guard and Bastion. But here in the financial district, it's all Bastion. For the moment, all the banks and financial offices in Brickell have chosen to stay in the city. So there are still thousands of people doing billions of dollars worth of business in Brickell. They have enough money to hire Bastion for their highest level of protection, which basically means buying your own small army and intelligence service. Honestly, they're probably safer now than they were before Miami fell to Florence.

We had a tense encounter with them on our first day in the city. A large black speedboat carrying half a dozen men in black body armor stopped us on the way into Brickell. We must have looked like squatters to them because they took one look at us and sprang into action. Their boat turned sideways to block our passage and four of them held their assault rifles at low ready, watching us for any signs of aggression. One of them spoke to us on a bullhorn, telling us that this was a restricted area and we had to leave.

Jess was really eager to give him an earful, but we had agreed that Harold and I would be the two main negotiators with any armed groups. Luckily, Harold had the foresight to bring a bullhorn too. He informed the Bastion captain that we had been sent here by the owner of One Broadway. He also said that this is not a restricted area, and unless these men were duly deputized officers of the law, they had no business detaining people on a public street.

The Bastion captain looked very annoyed. He said that he was deputized and that he didn't like Harold's tone. Harold is a perfect gentleman, though, so his tone was very reasonable. The captain just wasn't used to anyone talking back to him. Harold asked who had deputized him and the captain said that it was the Miami Chief of Police. Then the captain asked why he should believe us that we had been sent here by a building owner. Harold replied by asking why we should believe the captain the he was deputized. Jess laughed out loud at that comment. I laughed a little too. It broke the tension. The captain just got really frustrated and told us he'd be keeping his eye on us. Then he motioned for his men to stand down and the boat started speeding away.

He has definitely been a man of his word. When we're out running errands, we often see him and his men giving us the stink eye. They even cruise by sometimes at night, shining their bright lights into our lower floors to see what we've been up to.

So what have we been up to?

The focus of our first week was renovations. The ground floor of One Broadway was still visibly damaged by the storm and the saltwater. Our first order of business was to remove anything that was clearly broken or too waterlogged to keep. Jess, Ermete, Harold, Murray, Jalen, and I spent a few hours on that first day knee-deep in the water, pulling out ruined furniture, boarding up broken windows, and so on. Shortly after we arrived, we unloaded our first batch of supplies and put them in what would quickly become our main office on the second floor. Then we started loading trash into the boat and made a few trips to a nearby parking lot that was being used as a dump site for nonhazardous waste. Eventually, we picked up Ten and the others and brought them to our new home.

The first night there was fun but a little scary at the end. The building was mostly empty, so we had our choice from any number of high-end, fully-furnished apartments. We could have each had a floor to ourselves, but instead we decided to stick to one floor for security reasons. Jess, Ermete, and I decided to bunk together. Tenalach and Harold shared the apartment next door. The rest split into two or three small groups. After setting up our sleeping quarters for the night, Harold and I decided to go door to door and visit all of the residents left in the building.

That was an interesting experience. There were only twenty-two residents left in the building, scattered across fourteen different floors. They were all what I would call wealthy — not billionaires, of course, but wealthy enough to consider the high rent here a minor detail. These were people who stayed in the city after Florence because they had some important job in finance, insurance, or real estate. They were polite, well-dressed even at home, young to middle-aged, mostly Latino, and glad to hear that the owner had sent someone to look over the building.

Of course, we didn't go into details about our full plans for the building. Keeping it short and simple may have helped with the warm reception. One step at a time.

After going door to door with Harold talking to residents, I caught up with Jess and Ermete out on the outdoor tennis court on a balcony a few stories up. It turns out that the little pizza place on the ground floor had somehow managed to reopen a few weeks after Florence hit, so they had gone downstairs and gotten a couple of pizzas. The three of us sat around for a long time eating pizza and talking philosophy and looking up at the stars. It was a good way to relax at the end of the day, and we've done it several times since.

The scary part came in the middle of the night when we all heard gunfire. Unfortunately, it's not that uncommon to hear automatic weapons fire in the distance at night. It's still not safe out there at night. But the gunfire isn't really noticeable in our building. So when we heard that loud, distinctive, repetitive popping, we knew it was trouble, and we knew it was close.

Ermete grabbed a walkie-talkie while Jess and I looked out the window. As planned, we left this lights off so as not to attract attention. I felt vulnerable and a bit silly crouching by the window in my underwear in my dark, peeking outside to see what was happening. I couldn't see much from my angle, but it turns out that Bastion was having a gun battle with a handful of criminals who picked the wrong neighborhood to rob. The gunfire stopped after a few minutes. Harold told us over the walkie-talkie that two criminals had been killed, one Bastion had been wounded, and the rest of the criminals had fled for their lives.

Luckily, neither side drew us into the conflict. Still, though, the violence is disturbing. I'm not used to violence, not yet anyway. Ermete went back to sleep pretty easily, maybe because he has traveled to dangerous places before and is used to the danger. But Jess and I stayed up for a long time in the dark, talking in hushed tones about what had happened and how we felt about it. I actually don't remember falling asleep, which is rare for me. We just talked a long time until eventually we drifted off to sleep together on the couch.

That's probably the most violence we've had around here so far. Like I said, there's a good side to having so many Bastion in the neighborhood. They hassle us sometimes, which I'll talk about in more detail next time. But they also keep out other criminals. We hear commotion outside sometimes, but most criminals don't even try anything here because they know Brickell is off limits. Even the drug cartels don't want to push Bastion too hard out of fear of retaliation on their home turf overseas. If you think what Bastion does in the U.S. is bad, you should hear about what they do in other countries. I didn't even know it all until Jess started showing me the stories. I hope and pray that they don't ever start using those tactics here.

Not much else changed during our first week. We got everyone on the team moved into One Broadway, talked to the residents, did some basic cleanup and renovation, installed some rooftop solar using the solar modules we brought with us, and started meeting up with a few other people with similar interests. There were some struggles along the away, but given the fact that Miami is literally a disaster area, I feel like it went well.

PROTECTION RACKET
September 17, 2030 at 23:42

On our first day in Miami, Harold taught me a new term: protection racket.

A protection racket is when a criminal group offers to protect you from other criminals. You pay them some money, or give them something else they want, and they keep you safe. It's also sometimes a euphemism for an extortion racket. That's when they threaten to harm you unless you give them the protection money.

Bastion is running a protection racket in Miami, especially in and around Brickell. Unknown individuals or groups with a lot of money have hired a large number of Bastion troops to protect the banks and key financial offices in this neighborhood. This protection basically involves Bastion having a strong presence in the entire neighborhood — boat and foot patrols at all hours, armed guards stationed at certain buildings, surveillance on criminals to prevent any large coordinated assaults on Brickell, and so on. Because of this, they apparently feel entitled to squeeze protection money out of everyone who lives or works around here, including the dirt-poor greens who happen to have access to a luxurious residential skyscraper in Brickell.

It started with a sales pitch that almost seemed polite and professional. A day or two after we got here, they sent a thirty-something white woman in an expensive suit to come and speak with us. She pulled up to our door in a big white boat with half a dozen bodyguards in tow, talking to me and Harold at length about the protection services that Bastion offers. There are a few different tiers, each with its own benefits. She strongly recommended that we at least get the first tier, Basic Protection. As she told us about the benefits, she had this way of sounding very warm and caring while she was basically saying that we would all be abducted and killed by wild-eyed criminals if we didn't buy Bastion protection. I don't know if she believed her own sales pitch or she was just that good at sales. Either way, it was surreal.

As soon as she and her guards were out of earshot, I turned to Harold. I must have had an exasperated look on my face because he just laughed when he saw it. I laughed a little too, but then I had to say out loud what we were both thinking.

"Not a chance in hell, right?"

"You've got that right."

He burst out laughing again, and I found myself laughing with him. On some level, it really wasn't funny. This could be a life and death situation, after all. But that's why we had to laugh.

So far, life without Bastion protection has been okay. We had a few break-ins on the ground floor, so that was a little scary. But each time, it was just a couple of people trying to break in and rob the place. We had guards posted while the rest of us slept, so the robbers were chased off pretty easily. Harold and his Green Guard friends are very friendly, but they can also be very intimidating when they're decked out in camo body armor and carrying assault rifles. I know them well now and even I wouldn't want to sneak up on them while they were on duty.

At one point, the captain we met on our first day — who we now call Captain Hassle because he's always hassling us and that's how brilliant we are with nicknames — stopped our boat again and insisted that we needed to pay some protection money. It was just me, Ten, Lou, and Mel coming back from a trip to the park where some volunteers are busy dealing with all the dead trees and plants and discussing what to replace them with. It was still daylight out, so we were very relaxed until Captain Hassle came along, like a troll under a bridge demanding his toll.

I picked up the bullhorn and replied to him that we weren't going to pay. He said that we must be criminals if we didn't want to pay. Maybe our boat was stolen, or our guns, or our solar panels. I insisted that we would not pay and that we would report him to the police if he kept harassing us. That made everybody on his boat laugh. Then he said something that took me by surprise.

"Who do you think protects the police?"

That made my heart race a bit. I didn't even realize why until I thought it through. I knew that the police were struggling to fight all of the crime in the city and not having much luck with it. But it hadn't occurred to me that the police might need protection services from Bastion. The National Guard was protecting the city government itself, and that probably included the Chief of Police. But they weren't protecting all of the individual police officers out on the streets trying to do their jobs. So maybe that fell on Bastion.

Were the police paying protection money to Bastion? ¡Dios mío! What a mess.

I spent a while just thinking about that. Everything got quiet. Eventually, Captain Hassle spoke again.

"Now you understand the situation. If you don't have the cash, get the cash. Or get something else we need. Guns, ammo, gold, silver, good food. Burgers and brats and beer, not this [blanking] Miami [blank]. And the pizza place doesn't count! We made a deal with them before you [blanks] showed up. Don't make me ask you again, green."

After that little speech, he sped off to continue his patrol. Harold says that they probably won't bother attacking us because we have enough guns and not enough goods to steal. But ever since that conversation with Hassle, we've increased our security just to be sure.

That's about all I have time for tonight. Jess, Ermete, and I are all out on that tennis court again, as we often are on clear nights. There are some lights in the city, especially in Brickell, but it's not as bright as it used to be. If you look up at the night sky, you can see the stars. At the end of a long day, we often come out here to talk awhile and eat some cheap food that we bought or scavenged or traded for. But we tend to wake up at the crack of dawn nowadays, so we also go to bed much earlier than we used to. Ermete is already asleep in a chair and Jess just finished working on that Adventures in Global Warming game for the night. So it's time for me to get going too. Next time, though, I'll talk more about the projects we've been working on. I've been emailing a few of our supporters in Southern Illinois about these projects, but now I'm excited to talk about them on the blog. In the meantime, let me say again that if you're in Miami and you're working on anything remotely green-related, let me know. Maybe we can work together.

The Synergists
September 21, 2030 at 22:55

After two weeks in Miami, we finally came up with a name for our group: The Synergists.

It took us a long time because we all have such different ideas and opinions. Most of the names suggested by our Green Guard members sounded militaristic — things like Eco Squad, Green Battalion, and The G-Team, which apparently is a reference to a TV show called The A-Team that Harold watched as a kid. Jess liked that one because it was a pop culture reference. Tenalach, on the other hand, tended to come up with mystical-sounding names: the Atlanteans, the Reclaimers, the Renewers, the Green Nexus. Ermete and McKenna, the civil engineer I never did introduce properly here, had a few philosophical names in mind: Ecosophy, The Integralists, InteGreen, Greenaissance, Greenewal.

We chose The Synergists for a variety of reasons. The biggest one was the influence of Buckminster Fuller, a 20th century philosopher, architect, designer, inventor, and futurist whose insights and innovations served as inspiration for many green, holistic, and integral movements. Most of the people on our team are from Southern Illinois, and Bucky lived and taught in Southern Illinois for part of his life. I visited his geodesic dome museum while I was in Carbondale and I was really impressed by what I learned about him. And while we draw on other sources of inspiration too, his concept of synergy is a good description of what we're trying to do here. We're bringing together diverse groups of individuals and resources in order to achieve new and exciting things that none of them could achieve separately.

I also really like one of the quotes from his "World Game":

"Make the world work, for 100% of humanity, in the shortest possible time, through spontaneous cooperation, without ecological offense or the disadvantage of anyone."

That's a really big task, but hopefully our small actions here in Miami will be in line with that goal.

So what have we been working on?

It started with our own space. Over the past two weeks, we've been slowly but surely transforming One Broadway into a green living center. The roof at the very top of the building has been covered with solar modules and a rainwater catchment system. We haven't had a really good storm yet, but when we do, the rainwater will be collected in a few large containers on the upper floors and delivered by a gravity-fed system to the lower floors, mostly through existing plumbing. If residents want to drink it, they should filter it to be on the safe side. But it should be fine for showering, washing dishes, flushing toilets, and so on.

Toilets are actually one of the biggest problems in Miami today. Before Hurricane Florence, the sewer system was already in serious trouble, constantly working against the increasing frequency and severity of flooding to clear out the excess water. But now that most of the city is permanently flooded, the sewer is essentially useless. So what do we do with all of that sewage?

It depends on what neighborhood you live in.

If you live in a poorer neighborhood, there's nobody there to set up new systems to replace the flooded sewers,. There's also nobody to enforce any rules or laws about proper disposal of sewage. So you get some people just dumping buckets of human waste into floodwaters when no one's looking. That's just gross! Not a good solution. But honestly, what else can they do? There are these boats cruising around the city with portable toilets, but you have to pay to use them, and you're not allowed to bring in buckets of extra waste.

The richer neighborhoods like Brickell have strict enforcement of no-dumping rules, so the waters are a little cleaner here. The banks and offices hire waste management contractors who have set up a few different types of systems. I've heard that it usually involves either the wealthy equivalent of a Port-a-Potty or expensive modifications to the plumbing so that they just flush as usual and the waste all gets stored and shipped away in big containers.

It all seems to be working better than it did when I left the city in the aftermath of the storm. But the solutions for poor people are a mess, and the solutions for rich people involve a lot of needless waste of energy and money.

We can do better.

I'll admit that I didn't think much about toilets and sewage until I came back to Miami, but I've learned a lot in the past couple of weeks. There are things like composting toilets that can take care of human wastes without wasting so much water. And even if you do use a flush toilet, there are ways to waste less water and use biological processes instead of chemicals to clean it all.

There's no "away" or "elsewhere" for us to dump this water. We need to either not use water or set up ways to clean the water when we're done with it.

Since basic sanitation is such a big need, that's one of the first big projects we're working on outside of One Broadway. The Liminals are helping us to connect with other groups in Miami and resources outside of the city. Our long-term goal is to get each house — or at least each block — set up with its own way of treating human waste using either composting toilets or a variety of ecological wastewater treatments that use plants and microorganisms to clean the water.

I'm glad Jess and Ermete have such a good sense of humor about all of this. Tenalach is a permaculturist, so she's used to all of this talk about how to handle human waste in a green way. But it's very new to most of us, and honestly it was a little gross for me to think about at first. But Jess and Ermete lighten the mood with jokes about our glamorous new lifestyle here in Brickell, living in fancy apartments and installing solar panels and talking about [blank] all day. We're living the dream!

Another fun project we've been working on is gardening. Gardening takes time to set up, but we're getting it started. We're converting the rooftop tennis court and pool into outdoor garden spaces, and we're using some of the apartments that face in the right direction as greenhouses. The goal of these greenhouses will be to grow as much food as possible for the people who live here as well as some for trade.

One of the sad projects we've been working on is dealing with the effects of the saltwater on the trees. There's a park just across the corner from us called Simpson Park Hammock. Before Florence, it was already starting to suffer from saltwater stress caused by repeated flooding. Now, there's standing saltwater from the ocean throughout the park. There are still some people taking samples, measurements, and so on, but there's not much they can do for the park. Anything that can't handle saltwater is dead. All that's left to do is deal with the dead and dying plants and decide what if anything we want to replace them with.

We've only been here for about two weeks, so everything but the basic upgrades to One Broadway is still in the very early stages. We've been spending a lot of time lately meeting new people, finding out what projects they're working on, sometimes connecting people with each other, deciding what to focus on, and so on.

Honestly, my portion of it all is a lot more bureaucratic than I expected it to be. As the team coordinator, I have to keep track of who's working on what, why they're working on it, who they're working with, and so on. So I meet with people, prepare agendas, take notes, make spreadsheets, write emails, and so on. It probably sounds boring to some people, but to me it's very exciting. I spend all day meeting with friends, talking to new people, helping to plan green projects, and going on errands in our little speedboat, the Clover. That's always fun. I'm starting to get used to the fact that most of our travel nowadays is by boat rather than car, bus, or train. But on some level, it still feels strange and exciting to cruise down city streets in a speedboat.

I'm sure I'll have more news to share on these and other projects soon. In the meantime, Jess is going door to door and telling everyone on the team that Ermete has tracked down enough rum and fresh mint to make us all some proper mojitos. I was planning on going to bed now, but I may have to take some time first to celebrate his discovery. After all, no matter how hard we work, we have to remember to celebrate.

EXPANSION
September 26, 2030 at 23:42

What a week! It hasn't even been a full week since my last post, but it feels like it's been forever. I should post here more often. But so much is happening that I get caught up in it all and hardly find the time to write about it. We're trying to make history here, so I really should be doing a better job of keeping a written history. Harold says that's how it always is with "activist types" — too busy working to document the history of their own movements. I didn't used to think of myself in that way, but I guess watching my city sink beneath the waves had an effect on me. Spending time with Jess and Ermete had that effect on me too. Jess tends to be more political, but both of them are always thinking in terms of how to fix broken systems and create new systems that actually meet people's needs. It inspires me to do the same.

Now that we have our group name, we've decided to rename the building. One Broadway is now officially known as Synergy Central. The original owner supports the name change and has even started getting more involved with Miami Diaspora. It took some time to convince him because getting involved with Miami Diaspora is seen as very political. But he's seen what we're doing here and is fully supportive.

So what are we doing here?

The biggest news at our newly-christened Synergy Central is expansion. We have to be slow and careful about expansion because our resources are very limited and we want to be sure we can feed everyone who comes here. But the building is mostly empty, and it will still be mostly empty once we finish converting some of the rooms into greenhouses and workshops. So we may as well fill up that extra space with people who can join us in our efforts!

Our recruitment focus right now is on people who have special skills and don't currently have a stable place to stay. Every day at noon, I spend an hour or two meeting with new people who want to join us. So far, we've had about twenty people apply and have accepted seven. We've been working with the Liminals to secure better access to outside sources of food so that we don't have to rely on a handful of overpriced food boats and renovated grocery stores. When we first got here, Jess went off on a big rant about how all the food sources left in the city were engaging in price gouging, which is apparently when you raise prices really high in order to take advantage of a bad situation like the flooding of Miami. Sure, it costs a lot more than it used to for them to bring food into the city. But it's gotten to the point where even some simple dry beans that used to cost five or six dollars a pound now cost twenty or thirty dollars a pound. We can barter for some things, but usually not food. Thank God the pizzeria downstairs gives us a couple of free pizzas every week. I'm not as crazy about pizza as Jess is, but it's good to eat something other than beans and rice and scavenged canned vegetables.

We've also started what may be one of our most important projects right now.

The SmartBuoy system was Ermete's idea. It's a surprisingly cheap and durable little solar-powered buoy that floats around the edges of the flooding. It measures how deep the water is and has a little electric motor that it uses to move around and find the points where the water is getting too shallow for boats. That way, we won't have so many boats getting temporarily stranded or damaged because they went down the wrong street and started scraping bottom.

It's going to be a great system. Ermete has already built the first three prototypes and deployed them not far from here. He calls them his "smart boys" and dresses them in cute little raincoats and hats before setting them loose. They have simple AI that allows them to communicate with his tablet to share their location and a few other things. He can give them commands to change depth, move, take a nap, or make their way home.

In the short term, it doesn't really seem like that big of a deal. People seem to think of it as Ermete's pet project that he's doing for fun. But the goal is to get funding from the city and maybe private investors in order to deploy a whole fleet of SmartBuoys. They would make travel in and around the city go more smoothly. Online mapping programs aren't very helpful anymore because they don't show you the water depth on city streets. But this would allow us to see the water depth in real time and plot a course that suits the size of your boat. Ermete believes that information should be free, so as long as somebody can pay us for the actual buoys, the labor, and so on, then everyone in the city will have free access to these helpful tools.

That's some of the biggest news. On a less happy note, our little speedboat, Clover, was damaged by gunfire. On Monday night, someone shot out half of the windshield and damaged the hull with automatic weapons fire. They didn't damage the motor or batteries, thank God. We always keep the boat parked within site of our guards when we're not using it, but someone was bold enough to zip down South Miami and open fire on the boat in full sight of the guards. They got away, of course, because why would we expect someone to do a drive-by on our boat in the middle of the night? That's just crazy. We were able to patch up the damage to the hull, but we still haven't replaced the left windshield. It's not essential enough to be worth the trouble at this point.

So who did it? Your guess is as good as mine. It may have been Bastion trying to get across the idea that we need protection. Or it may have actually been some criminals who don't like what we're doing and know that Bastion isn't protecting us. Either way, it's not a very comforting thought. This time it was just vandalism, but it was vandalism with guns. It might escalate. We're peace-loving people, but we will defend ourselves if necessary. If it comes to that, I'm really not looking forward to it. But we will do it. We will protect ourselves and our home.

Anyway, whoever it is, I'm not going to let it get to me. We've got a good thing going here and won't be intimidated so easily. Hopefully if we keep growing in numbers and keep helping our neighbors, we'll get a good reputation. Maybe even the criminals will leave us alone. I don't know if it necessarily works like that, but we can always hope.

HURRICANE MICHAEL
October 2, 2030 at 21:42

Hurricane Michael just made landfall in New York. I'll keep this short because the news is still unfolding, but I have to post something.

Michael officially made landfall over an hour ago. They were expecting a serious storm, so a lot of people made preparations, including emergency responders, National Guard, and so on. But they weren't expecting a storm like this.

The intensity of the storm increased dramatically in the final hours before it made landfall. It also changed course, making a sharp turn to slam right into New York Harbor. They've taken many short-term and long-term measures to prepare for such storms, but there's simply no preparing for something like this.

The results of the course change and intensification were disastrous. Michael hit just about the worst possible spot with maximum intensity. Grid power is out in much if not most of the city. There's dramatic flooding radiating out from the harbor and running along the coasts. Subways, tunnels, and streets have been flooded, bringing everything to a halt.

When I started writing this, it was just me and Jess watching it all together on Jess' tablet. But then she ran up and down the hall knocking on doors and telling everyone about the news. Now there are about a dozen people and growing in our apartment, all of us crowded around a single tablet. Ermete is setting up a small projector so that we can all watch it on a wall together. There's a lot of discussion, but most of it is quiet and tense, talking in hushed tones and sharing moments of silence as we pore over live video and text feeds for the latest information. It will take days and weeks for the details to emerge, but we know that we're witnessing something historic, something catastrophic, something that resonates with us so strongly that there are no words to express it.

New York City is underwater.

It won't be permanent. The ground under New York City is very different than the porous limestone under South Florida. They also have much better elevation in New York and have spent the past ten or fifteen years building walls, elevated parks, berms, flood barriers, and other protective features. Honestly, all of that may have saved the city. But nothing could spare it entirely from a direct hit by a Category 5 hurricane. Many people have died and many more have been displaced. It's going to take months and probably even years for the city to recover.

But I worry about the recovery. The phrase "new normal" comes to mind. When I was growing up, they used that phrase all the time in discussions about global warming. Climate patterns are shifting dramatically due to human actions. It's not just about the heat we've added to the atmosphere and water, as bad as that is. So many other complex changes have taken place as a result of that. Melting ice, sea level rise, acidic oceans, and major shifts in the once-stable circulation of air and water around the globe. It would take a climatology degree to explain the nuances, but the broad strokes picture is clear to everyone who's not bought off by the fossil fuel industry. All of that disruption adds up to a climate that is fundamentally different than the one we evolved in. We're still struggling to understand the finer points of this new climate. What used to be considered an extreme weather event a few years ago is now considered the "new normal", a predictable part of our new climate patterns. And as I watch what's happening in New York City right now, I can't get that phrase out of my head.

New normal, new normal, new normal. Is this the new normal?

I need some fresh air now. I'm going to go up on the roof and stare out at the ocean for a while. I'll write again soon.

THE NEW NORMAL
October 4, 2030 at 21:26

After writing my last post, I spent a long time on the roof looking out at the ocean.

We live close enough to the coast that I could actually see the vast expanse of ocean that lies beyond the shining steel towers of the city. Given how late at night it was, there wasn't much to see. It was a dark, churning expanse of water, tossing and turning with the wind and tide, filling the air with a distinctive salty mist that always reminds me that the ocean is near.

Since we live so close to the coast, I could also turn in the other direction and see the vast expanse of the city stretching as far as the eye could see. It, too, was mostly dark, dotted with countless small points of light that only seemed to highlight the shadows that now engulfed the once-brilliant skyline. The sight of it all reminded me that this is a part of the ocean now too. It just happens to be a part of the ocean that has a lot of formerly-dry buildings in it.

As I looked back and forth between the east and west horizons, I had a realization. I can't really put it into words, but I'll try.

I tend to be an upbeat and positive person, finding the bright side of everything. But sometimes, just like anybody else, I need a good cry. As I looked out on the ocean — the old and the new — I cried for a while. I cried for all the people in New York who had died in Hurricane Michael, and the people in Miami who had died in Hurricane Florence, and all of the people in places I've never been who were suffering flood, droughts, wars, famines, and other consequences of global warming.

After crying for a few minutes, a great peace came over me. Jess came out to stand with me, resting her head on my shoulder quietly and looking out across the waves. Eventually, Ermete joined us too. We stood together in silence, looking at the ocean for a while before talking about what had happened and what it meant.

I eventually realized that "the new normal" wasn't just something that described the shift in climate patterns. More and more, with each passing day, it also describes the shift in human patterns.

Global warming isn't some type of accident of nature, like an earthquake or lightning or meteor strike. It's the result of human activities — our way of thinking, our way of living, certain systems of economic and political power that drive us to keep seeking endless profit, endless power, endless consumption, no matter the cost to humans and our planet's life support systems.

Our attitudes and our systems of power have created this "new normal", this climate that is much less conducive to human life than the old one. But as more and more people start to understand and accept what's happening, there's another type of "new normal" emerging. It's the "new normal" of resilience and resistance.

As I stood out on the roof with Jess and Ermete, talking philosophy and politics until the first hints of dawn, this was mostly just an idea. I looked out on the ocean to the east and the Ocean City to the west, and I realized that what we're doing in Miami is really just the start of "the new normal" for humans — a new way of living, a new way of resilience and resistance, a new way of social change that is just as disruptive to our social and economic infrastructure as the storms are to our physical infrastructure.

As we change the climate, the climate changes us. Every person displaced by climate change can become an agent of social change. And together, we will establish a "new normal" that would have seemed impossible just a few years ago. We will stop using fossil fuels; we will have a carbon negative economy; we will prepare for the changes in the climate that are already locked in; and we will work together to make it all happen. All nine billion of us.

I was finally able to get to sleep in the early morning hours with that comforting thought on my mind. I didn't get a chance to post about it yesterday because we were busy working and watching the latest updates from New York City — much of the city underwater, in some places up to the second or third floor, many hundreds lost, many thousands displaced, streets and subways flooded, all Northeastern states in a declared state of emergency. You've seen the news, you know what's happening.

But today, during and after a good day's work, there was also some very encouraging news.

People are finally getting it. After spending my whole life learning about global warming, and watching corrupt politicians and greedy businessmen push ahead full speed with fossil fuels, I saw something amazing. Spontaneous demonstrations in just about every major city in the U.S. and many others around the world. Millions of people suddenly in the streets with no planning or organizing. And they're not just protesting. They're asking what they can do. They're holding neighborhood meetings in the parks, streets, parking lots, malls, schools, abandoned buildings, any place they can. They're making plans for relief projects in New York, relief projects in other countries, resilience projects in their own communities, resistance campaigns in their own regions. Global warming is shifting from being a vague political idea to being their top concern. And they're raising hell about it.

Honestly, part of the reason I didn't post yesterday and barely posted today is because it's happening here too. Here in Miami, a city freshly swept beneath the waves, where many people still have no electricity, little food, and are going to the bathroom in buckets, there was an outpouring of support in response to Michael. A large group of people who have heard about the work that we're doing gathered right at the edge of Brickell, as far as Bastion would let them go. There were hundreds of them, some in small inflatable rafts, some in small boats, some in inner tubes, many just wading through the floodwaters. They all wanted to come to Synergy Central and do what they can to help, both here in Miami and off in New York if they can find a way there.

I rode out in our speedboat with Harold and Tenalach to meet them. We formed a three-person executive committee for the Synergists recently, and we decided it was best to have the whole committee present for something as big as this.

The first thing we had to do was lead the crowd away from the growing number of Bastion troops amassing at the edge of Brickell. A very uptight group of forty or fifty young men in black body armor was getting ready to disperse the crowd with guns and gas. Once we were a safe distance from the Bastion troops, we talked for a few hours with the people in the crowd. Some of them were lifelong community organizers, but most were just people who were eager for change and ready to do whatever they could to make it happen.

We weren't really ready to absorb so many new people so quickly. So we eventually came to a compromise.

We decided to take in a few dozen new people at Synergy Central. But we would also help set up two smaller Synergy centers in two other parts of the city. Some people talked about a long-term goal of setting up a Synergy center in every neighborhood. I really like that idea. But that's a lofty long-term goal. In the meantime, we'll work with what we've got. One location at Synergy Central, and hopefully two new locations in other neighborhoods within the next week or two.

There was also a small group of people who were adamant about going to New York City to help with the relief effort. We tried to explain that getting a couple dozen low-income people that far away and giving them enough supplies to make a difference is pretty much impossible given the current circumstances in Miami. But they insisted. So I called the Liminals and asked if these volunteers could use the big old electric bus that we drove here from Southern Illinois. After some negotiating, they said that the relief team could take the bus as far as Atlanta if they were willing to have a few people take supplies from Atlanta back to Miami while the rest made their way to New York City by other means.

And so, less than forty-eight hours after Hurricane Michael made landfall, the sunken city of Miami organized two new resilience and resistance centers and made plans to send a relief team up to New York City. The new Synergy centers will probably just start out as empty rooms or buildings, and the relief team will probably just have a small amount of non-perishable food and some water purifiers and tools and a couple of inflatable rafts. But given the circumstances, that's pretty amazing.

This is the new normal. Yes, the new normal for the climate is very bad. It's going to displace billions of people within my lifetime. It's a global catastrophe, and even if we make really good choices from this point forward, we can't avoid it entirely. But the new normal for humanity is starting to look good. More and more people are deciding to work together to make things better.

If we keep this up, maybe we won't even need the old systems anymore. We can just create new systems from the ground up. I just met in a general assembly with a few hundred people, people from all types of different beliefs and backgrounds, and it only took us a few hours to figure out dozens of complex and difficult problems. It's not perfect, but it's better than leaving everything up to the rich people who hired Bastion, or the city and state politicians who are just guarding their own buildings right now, or the gangs who are taking advantage of the situation. And the more people who get involved, the more it seems like we really can make the needed changes together.

I've got a very busy few days ahead of me. It's going to take time and energy to train all of these new people, especially the ones who will be starting the two new Synergies. A lot of that training will be done by other people, but I need to get it started since it involves creating new centers and coordinating communication and travel between them. Busy, busy, busy. It's a good type of busy, though. I may not post again for a few days while we work on all of this, but I'll post again as soon as I get the chance. I'm sure there will be plenty of news to share.

SYNERGY
October 7, 2030 at 23:42

First, let me start with the bad news, which is of course the updates from New York metropolitan area. I won't go into much detail because there are so many other people writing about it who know so much more than I do. But given how related it is to our own struggles here in Miami, and the struggles of people in other coastal cities around the world, I have to at least say something.

New York City has done more adaptation and mitigation than Miami because of the different political climate. We were more vulnerable in Miami, but some of our politicians and business leaders were too proud to admit that our city was slowly but surely slipping into the sea. We really did try to adapt, but politics slowed down our transition. New York City went in the opposite direction and spent the past ten or fifteen years increasing their emphasis on clean energy and climate adaptation. Politics slowed down their transition too, of course, but not as much.

When you consider the fact that they're the most populous metropolitan area in the U.S., New York City has a surprisingly high percentage of clean energy. This is mostly because they resisted the temptation to get drawn into the horrors of fracking. While some states were doubling down on fossil fuels in the form of fracking, the State of New York had a moratorium on fracking. That was when the fracking industry learned that poisoning the water of millions of New Yorkers was much harder than poisoning the water of millions of scattered and disempowered rural people in other parts of the country. So the frackers moved on to invade other states, leaving poisoned water, high cancer rates, earthquakes, and so on in their wake. Meanwhile, New York had to get its energy from somewhere, and coal was on the way out, so they went with clean energy. It was really a win-win for them, while all of the areas that chose fracking were left in a hot mess of poverty and pollution once the fracking bubble burst.

Even though New York City wasn't fully prepared for that storm in particular — who could be? — they were prepared for storms in general. So that makes it much easier for them to gather data about the aftermath of the storm and deploy resources where available and necessary.

The official death toll of Hurricane Michael is currently at 950 who died during the storm itself and another 350 who have died during the aftermath, leading to a total death toll of 1300. For better or worse, all this surveillance we're under nowadays makes it easier to count the casualties, even when rescue crews haven't had time to find the body. If your phone records show that you were in a building when it was destroyed by the storm, for example, it's safe to count you among the casualties unless you miraculously show up at an emergency shelter.

The damage is spread out over the whole metropolitan area and beyond. The storm itself affected a large area, and now the displacement of a massive number of people at once is creating all sorts of secondary problems. They have no quick and reliable way to calculate the number of displaced. They estimate that tens of thousands of people are very likely to face long-term displacement and ten times as many face short-term displacement. But that's assuming that basic services like electricity, water, sewer, and so on get fixed in a reasonable amount of time. It could be more. Large portions of the city are still dark at night because a lot of the solar power comes from the big solar plants that feed into the grid and the grid is having a lot of problems right now. But some buildings have lights because they have solar or other backup power.

On the plus side, as I said earlier, they've prepared for this. They have plans. Lives are being saved by their extensive preparations. It's estimated that the storm wall and related features saved over a thousand lives, cutting the casualty rate in half. Whatever politicians approved that project are probably going to be re-elected for as long as they want. They're also trying to move the displaced toward various emergency shelters set up by the city and FEMA, although it's very difficult with all of the flooding. Special pumps are working nonstop to clear the streets, tunnels, and subways, but when a storm surge submerges large portions of your city under 10 or 15 feet of water, it takes time to clear it all out. They're using boats and helicopters to do disaster relief in the many areas that still can't be reached by buses and vans and such.

So that's the latest news about the situation in New York. Now, I'd like to get back to the situation in Miami.

The situation in Miami is so much better than the situation in New York right now. I know it may not seem that way at first. The City of Miami is still mostly underwater, of course, and there are a lot of people who are still struggling to survive. The gangs and mafias control parts of the city without any objection from the police or Bastion. Most people who lived here prior to Hurricane Florence are still either a refugee out in the world somewhere or a refugee right here in the city, squatting wherever they can find shelter and doing their best not to cross paths with the many different types of armed enforcers roaming the streets at night.

But look at it this way. The city is on the mend. Miami is in the early stages of a renewal that could serve as a model for all major cities overwhelmed by the ocean. We have well-established and sensible rules for traveling by boat through the flooded parts of the city. We have stopped wasting money on fighting the ocean and started rebuilding ourselves as a smaller, leaner, but more sustainable Ocean City. A small but steady stream of people are contacting Miami Diaspora seeking reintegration into the city. Most of them — most of us, I should say — want to help turn Miami into a regional if not global model of climate adaptation and resilience.

Honestly, I almost feel a certain guilt about how well things are going here while all of those people in New York and surrounding areas are swept up in such a devastating and all-too-familiar tragedy. But I'm happy that things are improving here.

The City of Miami has expressed its support for Ermete's SmartBuoy system. Now he's working with some of our newest members to speed up the manufacturing process. We don't have the resources or demand to do any type of industrial-scale manufacturing, but Ermete has put together a small team of people to scavenge or trade for the simpler parts, put the buoys together, and deploy them where the city wants them. It's really exciting to see Ermete's plan become such a successful reality. And the city has connected us with a funding source for the SmartBuoys, so we have enough money to buy most of the expensive parts (solar modules and IT hardware) and keep the rest of it as profit so that we can actually feed ourselves.

Getting in the city's good graces also makes me feel a little more comfortable about Bastion, who have been increasingly hostile toward us as we increase our numbers and work more closely with other people outside of Brickell. They see us as a dangerous influence in what used to be a tightly controlled stronghold of the big banking interests remaining in the city. Of course, I'm sure that won't stop them from taking advantage of their free access to the Smart Buoy system. They complain about us, but they'll use our tech when it serves them.

In other good news, we've also started setting up the two other Synergy Centers.

Synergy Central, formerly known as One Broadway, will probably always be our main base of operations. The layout of this building is a bit odd for us since it's mostly segmented into individual apartments. We've had to repurpose some of these apartments to be workshops, classrooms, storage areas, and of course greenhouses and indoor gardens. It's funny on some level to see fancy Brickell apartments being repurposed into Ermete's mad science workshop, and Harold and Tenalach's indoor gardening projects, and our own modest armory, and so on. But it works. We've filled almost the entire upper roof, tennis court, and swimming pool area with solar modules and a green roof filled with plant beds that capture and clean the rainwater. We've also added composting toilets in the building to make up for the fact that the sewers are basically out of commission for the foreseeable future. Once our gardens reach full capacity, we'll be able to feed and house fifty or more people in a carbon-negative building.

I've gotten really used to living at Synergy Central. This place is home to me now and I plan on staying here. But it's also good to see us expanding into two other locations. I haven't even been out to visit the other locations yet because they're basically just empty buildings at this point. But Jess and Harold have gone out with a few of our Green Guard members to check out the locations that our new team members in Little Havana and the Roads have picked out. They all agreed that the spots were decent, although no spot is ideal, especially since the whole city is still in a fair amount of fluctuation and chaos.

This is going to be a big change for us here at Synergy Central. There are already some new people filtering in from Synergy Havana and Synergy Roads, which is what we're calling the two locations until they get settled and possibly come up with more creative names. We're also sending out a few of our people to help them get settled, including a couple of our original team members: our plumber, Murray, and our jack-of-all-trades, Lou. Murray's skills are desperately needed by people working on new residential plumbing systems, including setting up rainwater catchment systems, graywater systems, and various types of low-flow or no-flush toilets. Lou just likes a challenge and is traveling between the two new centers to do odd jobs and teach martial arts, including basic gun safety and use. They were both big helps around here and their presence will be sorely missed. But I'm sure they'll be a big help out there, and new people are coming in to fill some of the roles they used to fill.

Jess says that Synergy Central and the two new Synergies are all becoming one big social experiment. I hadn't thought about it that way, but I see what she means. This is what she's come out here to study for her degree – how people from different cultures and backgrounds can work together on climate adaptation and mitigation projects. How do their different cultural backgrounds and economic situations inform their approach to the work? How do they work together across social and economic lines? What barriers do they encounter and how do they work through them? She spends most of her time doing various types of practical work like the rest of us, but she also spends a few hours each week interviewing people, taking notes, and so on. It will take her a while to do the research, but since she's right here in the middle of it all, I'm sure it'll be very exciting research. I talk to her about it about once a week, and I'm looking forward to reading it someday, once it's published and everything settles down. If everything ever settles down.

Here I am writing all night when I should be sleeping! I have to be up at six in the morning and it's almost midnight. Oh well. No rest for the wicked, as they say. I didn't even get around to talking about the upcoming elections. Hopefully I'll get to that tomorrow. If not, I'm sure I'll post again soon. So much is happening that it sometimes keeps me away from this blog for a few days. But then again, so much is happening that I have to keep writing about it. Somebody has to tell the story.

OCTOBER SURPRISE
October 9, 2030 at 22:15

We've been really busy for the past few days helping our newest Synergist recruits set up Synergy Havana and Synergy Roads. Each center is facing its own challenges, but so far it's nothing too serious. They're both working with neighborhood associations, so they both have some volunteers and material resources to draw on. Ever since Hurricane Florence, these neighborhood associations have played a major role in organizing the neighborhoods in the absence of outside help. Both groups have enough resources to start a basic center and get a few projects going. But Havana is starting out with some serious supply shortages and Roads is short on volunteers, especially the volunteers they need to set up their new plumbing and food systems.

The simple solution would be to set up some type of simple exchange. Havana has a lot of people willing to work and Roads has a shortage of people and a surplus of supplies. But of course, life is not always simple. Miami still mostly functions based on the old economy — money, money, money. We're all part of one team now, so we don't want to turn this into an impersonal business transaction. But we've only been on the same team for a few days, so people are wary of donating a bunch of work or goods to virtual strangers.

Even with the ocean lapping at our feet — and our knees, and our waists — we have to deal with the same old money problems. In our case, though, it's getting easier. The two neighborhoods as a whole aren't on the same page, but our new Synergist recruits all support the idea of finding cooperative solutions and creating new green projects to help the people of Miami. So the solution here shouldn't be too difficult. I've been involved in some back and forth discussions to set up a basic sweat equity system. People who work for a neighboring Synergy Center earn volunteer hours that can be traded in for resources like food, tools, supplies, and so on. It's an inexact science, and we're basically just helping each other out because we all share similar goals of rebuilding Miami in a green way. But a sweat equity system like this helps people who still think of things in terms of exchanging labor for goods and vice versa.

Life at Synergy Central has been very busy. But now that these other two centers are starting to gather their own momentum, I've had time to take a good look at what's going on nationally. And it's big.

Honestly, the whole world is in a big state of upheaval right now. Thailand, Bangladesh, Japan, and a few other places have been hit by superstorms again. Coastal cities around the world are experiencing record flooding. Inland cities are experiencing a flood of refugees from the coasts and the rural areas devastated by droughts. It's too much for me to take in at the end of a long, hard day of work. But looking at the national level is a bit more reasonable to me — something I understand, something I can process, something I can maybe even be a part of in my own small way.

The United States is still one of the largest emitters of greenhouse gases. If you count all the products we buy from China, really, we're the biggest emitters by far. Everybody knows this. We've known this for decades. But now, people in this country are really starting to understand it. They know it in their bones now. They know that when we flood the air with greenhouse gases, Miami goes underwater, and New York City goes underwater, and the plains of the Midwest and valleys of the West are stricken with drought, and so many other bad things start to happen.

And they're acting on it. Not just on some solemn day of action when we all march together to raise awareness. Millions of people are out on the streets of America every day now. I don't even think there's any one group — or five groups, or ten groups — organizing it. People just know to go out in the streets and see what they can do. The old Occupy groups have revived under several different names and styles, holding various types of general assemblies in public spaces to talk about resistance and resilience. In places that still rely heavily on dirty energy, they're making serious plans to stop all fossil fuel use by working together to install their own solar and wind immediately. Some of the bigger Green Front direct action groups like Rising Tide are suddenly organizing all types of massive sit-ins, lockdowns, and blockades in an effort to stop every fossil fuel project left in this country. Green Guard and other green militias are surging in membership as people prepare for the possibility of the government or corporations trying to stop all of this citizen action.

It's like nothing any of us have ever seen before. This is the most active I've seen people get in my entire life. Harold and Tenalach have been around for a lot longer than I have, and they say the same. It's different here in Miami because of how many people left the city. Just surviving here in a green way is its own small victory. But it's exciting to come home every night and see these images from all across the country — everyday people like me getting excited and working together to do what they can about the situation. I guess that our own big surge in Synergist membership is a part of that too.

It's even changing the course of this year's election. Before Florence and Michael, there was just the usual debate about whether or not the Democrats would succeed in retaking the House. You know what it's like. You've seen all the attack ads and the endless promises, billions of dollars spent to convince us to vote for the same people we always vote for. It's ridiculous. But now there's a tremendous outpouring of support for any candidate who advocates climate action and a huge backlash against anyone who opposes it. Some of the two-party candidates who were already strong on climate are doing well, but anyone who was on the fence or a climate science denier is taking serious losses right now. The pollsters and pundits say that if the election were held today, the Green Party would claim about a fourth of the House, a seat or two in the Senate, and a couple of Governor seats. The Climate Party would also possibly gain a few seats in the House. State-level races are being affected too. It's not exactly a revolution, but it would probably be enough to start pushing through some really strong climate legislation really quickly.

Some people are calling it the October Surprise. Since we have our elections in early November, there's often be something big and controversial that comes up in October that changes the course of an election. October Surprise is often a negative term, but in this case, it's turning out to be a good thing. We've had a few too many cases of climate disruption lately for people to be complacent anymore. We will not be silent. We will stand up and make the changes needed in the world today.

As positive as I try to be, I can honestly say that I find this huge wave of public support surprising. I wasn't doing much about the problem before Florence, and I figured most people wouldn't get active until their home went underwater too. But there they are, out in the streets, maybe a bit chaotic and confused, but doing their best to make it happen. This is one October Surprise that may change the course of history for the better. Here's hoping.

THE PURGE
October 12, 2030 at 02:42

Everything is crazy now. I don't know what to say.

Somebody didn't like the Green Front's October Surprise. So they came up with an October Surprise of their own. This one involved a lot of guns.

The premise, of course, was national security. Some of these climate demonstrations have been successfully shutting down our remaining fossil fuel infrastructure — export terminals, extraction projects, even a few power plants for short periods. The initial response by the government was the same as usual: detain some people, arrest others, basically just break up the demonstration and charge some small portion of the people with serious crimes.

But now they're treating this as a massive breach of national security. All hell has broken loose. They're in the process of a nationwide sting operation that has targeted the leadership of any group that they consider to be part of the Green Front. This has included some people like Deep Green Resistance who probably had serious mischief on their minds. But it has also included other people who don't even focus on any type of direct action or civil disobedience. Groups that work on clean energy, or resilience, or all types of other harmless things. But if they have ties to people who get arrested, or if they advocated any remotely militant form of protest, they're considered part of this alleged "conspiracy to disable American infrastructure".

You have to keep in mind here that Green Front is not an actual organization. There are dozens of unrelated groups that get lumped together under the banner of Green Front. Some of these groups even fight with each other about how to respond to global warming. It's just a general term that people have come up with to describe all individuals and groups that support some type of strong resistance to fossil fuels or radical changes toward a more ecological and community-oriented society.

But a lot of that is open to interpretation. Suppose I say that we must stop all fossil fuel use in order to avoid the most catastrophic responses to global warming. Is that a common sense science-based policy recommendation, or is that the statement of a wild-eyed Green Front radical who needs to be disappeared?

The current administration has decided to take a more hardline stance on this question in response to all of the demonstrations. In just the past 48 hours, thousands of people have been grabbed suddenly in no-knock raids — some conducted by law enforcement, some conducted by Bastion, all involving Homeland Security in some way.

It wasn't as successful as they planned. Here in Miami, they just didn't have enough boots on the ground to pull off a massive campaign like they did in other major cities. They tried something with Bastion, but I'll talk about that more in my next post. In other parts of the country, they had a lot more resources to work with. But still, the results were mixed. About a third of the people they were trying to arrest got away. Some of it resulted in violence because the government decided to conduct these no-knock raids on the homes or bases of armed Green Guard militias. At least a dozen law enforcement officers died and an estimated fifty or sixty of their targets died, although it's hard to be sure since some of them got away wounded.

It was a disaster. But it was also extensively organized, with coordinated raids in dozens of places within minutes of each other. This can't be something they thought of after Hurricane Michael and everything else started getting people out in the streets. It hasn't been long enough for them to plan something like this. This has to be something they've been planning for more than a few days — maybe months, maybe longer. They knew that sooner or later, we would all get fed up with the climate disruptions and the growing impacts it's having on our daily lives. So they came up with a plan. That plan apparently involved arresting as much of the leadership as possible and herding any remaining dissidents into refugee camps.

But it didn't work. This is a mostly leaderless movement. People are scared, but they're still out in the streets, probably still a few million across the country. Some cities are starting to declare curfews, disperse "unlawful assemblies", and so on. Numbers have dropped due to some people being arrested and some going home, but there are still plenty of people out there to make a difference. Here in Miami, each neighborhood has at least one big gathering where people are coming together to talk about it. Nobody knows what to do next, but everybody has an idea, and they're all talking.

Really, one of the most devastating long-term consequences of this "purge" may be the effect on the elections. For the first time that anyone can remember, the government has arrested a large number of political candidates and charged them all with conspiracy. This includes most of the Green Party candidates, all of the Climate Party candidates, and even a few Democrats who had a few too many Green friends. The President himself got on TV tonight to say that the arrests were not political — that these people were arrested because they had been actively working with individuals who intended to commit specific crimes to shut down critical infrastructure using civil disobedience and direct action.

But how can you arrest dozens of candidates, most of them from the same political party, and say it's not political?

The whole world seems to be holding its breath, waiting to see what happens here. The leaders of other countries are already talking about how to respond to what many see as election tampering. There are similar struggles going on in other countries too, some of them much more violent and oppressive than our own. But what happens here may have a major impact on the whole world.

Will we take action on global warming this time around or won't we? That's the big question. It doesn't look as promising after all of these arrests. That's going to put a serious damper on both the election and on all of the resilience and resistance projects that various groups are working on. But there are still a lot of people out in the streets, so it's still possible. I don't know what will come of it, but at least we're trying to make it happen.

BASTION STRIKES
October 13, 2030 at 12:34

I talked yesterday about the nationwide raids on people and groups that the government has identified as Green Front. Now let me tell you what happened here in Miami.

Obviously, the Synergists survived. I wouldn't be sitting here typing this message if we'd all been captured or killed. But the raids did do considerable damage.

Synergy Central was one of dozens of targets across the country that were hit at almost exactly the same time by anti-green forces. Depending on the resources available in each city (and a few rural areas), the teams consisted of some combination of local police, state police, Bastion, and some type of special forces that we think were directly overseen by some intelligence agency. The government is being very vocal about the need for these raids, but very quiet about the exact details. These special forces had no identification, of course, so we have no way of knowing who exactly they were.

If we had been a bigger target, we would all be in jail right now — or worse. The raids on the biggest targets were very successful because they had the most resources: communications monitoring and disruption, the new sonic cannons, knockout gas, armed drones, hundreds of troops, and so on. But we get the impression that the policy makers in Washington have written off Miami as a lost cause. So no federal troops or special ops teams for Miami. The remaining police in Miami are overwhelmed on a good day, and the Florida National Guard members who aren't overseas fighting for oil and natural gas are busy protecting key infrastructure. So they decided to let Bastion run the whole show here.

It was quite a show. Jess, Ermete, and I were all asleep in our apartment at Synergy Central. Harold was away visiting Synergy Roads for the night. Our exact head count at Central on any given night varies, but that night we had thirty-two people. Many were asleep like us, but some were awake on guard duty.

The local Bastion leaders must have thought that we were some type of helpless community center that hadn't put any thought into our defenses. About two dozen of them rolled right up to our front door in three black boats with all the lights turned off. Two of the boats unloaded their crew to storm the building on foot while the third boat hung back a bit so they could lob teargas and flashbang grenades into the first few floors. About a dozen other people went to other parts of the building to cover alternate exits. All of these people were in black tactical gear and had various tools and weapons to help them in the raid.

If we hadn't been prepared, it would have been easy for them. They had about as many people as us, if not more. They all had better gear and training than most if not all of us. They were all awake. They had the cover of darkness in their favor. It would have been a slam dunk if we weren't prepared.

But we were prepared.

From the outside, it looks like we just have two guards at night who are just casually watching TV and using the internet to pass the time. But really, we always have several more just out of sight. They're usually the people with the most experience. Harold and the other Green Guard have given us all at least some training, but our night guards tend to be ex-military. They have a lot of important skills related to security and know how to keep their heads in a crisis.

When Bastion lobbed a flashbang grenade through the front door, our team knew what to do. The two at the front desk were momentarily stunned, obviously, because that's what flashbang grenades do. But our backup team understood immediately what was happening and sprang into action. After a brief exchange of gunfire, our people sounded the alarm and retreated up the stairs. Once they made it up the first flight, one of them activated our first line of defense.

Ermete calls it the Zapper.

Like most buildings in Miami, the first floor of Synergy Central is always flooded. The water's low enough that we can still get in and out using the old doors. We can even put some desks and ramps on boosters to raise a portion of the ground floor above water. But even after that, most of our lobby is still flooded with water. So we decided to use that to our advantage. We wired the lobby so that with the press of a button, the whole thing becomes electrified. It took a couple of weeks of rewiring and testing, and it's an outrageous safety hazard and building code violation, but it works.

Most of the first wave of Bastion troops were subjected to a strong enough shock to cause a momentary paralysis, leaving them helpless and at risk of drowning. If it had been freshwater, it probably would have been lethal. As it was, Jalen and Bridget had to go back down into the lobby to make sure that no one was actually drowning. Of course, we took away their weapons too.

We were hoping that the Zapper would discourage any other troops from entering the building. Bastion troops are mercenaries, after all. They're not doing this out of some high-minded idealism about God and country. They're doing it for a paycheck. And that paycheck seems a lot less important when your buddies just got zapped downstairs.

Unfortunately, they were very determined. They made their way onto our lower level roof — the former pool and tennis court — by climbing over from a neighboring office building. They trashed part of our garden and damaged a rainwater catchment system along the way. Fortunately for us, we had already seen this coming. We changed all of the locks on those doors so that we could lock out any intruders who tried to come in that way. We go in and out of those rooms all the time during the day, but at night it's locked up tight. There's also additional reinforcement on the doors and a few barricades in the hallways on those floors. This slowed them down enough that we were able to drive them back out of the building with some of our own flashbang grenades and a few warning shots to let them know that we were armed.

Honestly, most of this happened before I was even ready. Our team downstairs sounded the alarm and triggered the Zapper, and the Green Guard among us who were asleep when it all started sprang into action a little faster than the rest of us. My role consisted of waking up, figuring out what the hell was happening, and running out the apartment door with Jess and Ermete to see how we could help. I ended up tossing a flashbang grenade down a tube to disorient the Bastion troops while Ermete talked on the walkie-talkie and Jess covered the door to make sure none of the Bastion troops had found a way to sneak up on us.

Ultimately, our defense of Synergy Central was successful. A few Synergists had minor injuries, including one of the lobby guards who was shot in the bicep and grazed in the head, which apparently bleeds a lot even when it's not a deep wound. Jalen and Bridget tended to the wounded, including some of the Bastion troops who had to be rescued from drowning and carried out to their boats under a white flag with a red cross on it. It was basically just a painted bedsheet, but it worked. Once their ground crew was mostly disarmed and their roof crew was on the run, they gathered up their wounded under our watchful eyes and beat a hasty retreat.

That was without a doubt one of the most stressful and scary and frustrating experiences of my life. I feel sick inside just thinking of it. I'm still not used to anything remotely resembling violence. It was loud and confusing and bloody and awkward and way too real. I spent most of my life completely removed from violence, and on some level I feel like the past couple of months of occasional training has not been enough to prepare me for the realities of living at constant risk of violence.

But you know what? I survived. And we survived. None of us died. None of us got captured. And we didn't lose our home. There's some damage, but we can repair it with time.

What we can't repair, I'm sure, is our relationship with Bastion. They were never happy to have us on the edge of their turf, but now they must want to drive us out of here by any means necessary. Hopefully the fact that we provided emergency care to over a dozen Bastion troops will help soften their hearts, but somehow I doubt it. The government will probably tell them to try again — and even if they don't, Bastion may take it upon themselves to try again just so that they can be rid of us.

With that in mind, I decided earlier tonight to send Bastion a warning.

We know about how many troops Bastion currently has in the Brickell area. If they really wanted to, they could definitely get together enough people to take us out. No contest. But you know what? It would leave them vulnerable. Very vulnerable. The only way they could put together a bigger raid would be to pull people off of their regular duty assignments — patrolling the streets of Brickell, guarding the banks and offices, doing personal security for the most rich and powerful people around here, and so on. So I decided to send them a warning.

If they attack us again, we'll send out a distress signal to the entire city. If we do that, two very important things will happen. The first is that our growing number of friends at Synergy Havana and Synergy Roads and the Liminals and beyond will each send some backup our way. The second is that every criminal organization in Miami will know that the banks and offices are vulnerable.

I don't like making these types of decisions. I don't like playing these types of games. I just want to be left in peace to spend time with my friends working on our ecological and community projects. But don't mistake this desire for peace as a sign of fear or weakness. If you come and attack a peaceful group of Synergists who are just trying to provide food and electricity and sustainable living to the people of this city, there will be consequences. You may take down Synergy Central, but you will lose Brickell. Keep that in mind the next time someone in Tallahassee or Washington or anywhere else tells you it's time to go attack a group of people who have never done you any harm.

So there it is. That's what happened here in Miami during the Purge, as some people are calling it. There were a few other small arrests, but their main attack failed. Here's hoping they'll have the good sense not to try again.

CALM BEFORE THE STORM
October 15, 2030 at 22:22

It seems like there's been a lot less chaos for the past day or two, both in Miami and in the rest of the country. But somehow, it feels like the calm before the storm.

Here in Miami, the city is remarkably calm. There's still the high crime rate in some areas, of course, and some areas entirely controlled by gangs. But no big street battles or massive public gatherings.

We're trying to get back into our daily routine here at Synergy Central. So far, there haven't been any reprisals from Bastion. They no longer patrol the street right in front of the building, but they do still patrol the cross streets, so we know they're out there. Watching, waiting. For what, I don't know. Maybe they're hunkering down and protecting their clients at the local banks, office, and mansions rather than harassing the local community organizers.

Our projects are going well. Now that we have a lot more people, we could really use a few more electric boats. We still have our first boat, the Clover, and another small boat that Ermete converted into an electric. But boats are hard to come by in this town, as you can imagine. They're all taken. So we end up running these boats about all day, moving around people and supplies as we make a few additions to Synergy Central and help Havana and Roads get more established.

Speaking of Ermete, his SmartBuoy system is working really well. He has a few volunteers making occasional tweaks to the hardware and software, adding new features as people who use the system request them. One of the buoys was vandalized, damaged beyond repair. But the vandals didn't realize that each buoy has a small camera. We posted a photo of the vandals online and haven't had any vandalism since. A lot of people are using the system now to help navigate the city, so most people seem content to leave them in peace.

Jess has been spending more time at Synergy Havana lately than she's been spending here! I miss her when she's away, but she's doing good work over there, teaching some classes and doing odds and ends like helping in the garden, light construction, cleaning, and so on. Her Spanish is getting much better! She even talks to me en español sometimes, which is nice.

Harold and Tenalach used to spend a lot of time together, but lately they hardly see each other. They both love gardening, so they still get to garden together sometimes. I just saw them out in the garden together when I visited Synergy Havana yesterday. But we have a lot of new people, and they have a lot to teach, so they spend most of their time teaching.

Harold teaches some people who are joining Green Guard and others who just want to know basic self-defense, basic gun training, and so on. Each Synergy base has a security coordinator now, so the three of them also meet at least once a week to talk shop. We're a very peace-loving group, but we are always mindful of the fact that we live in a flooded city where basic services like police and ambulances are still mostly lacking. We'd be eaten alive by local gangs and Bastion bounty hunters if we didn't have some type of defenses. They test those defenses from time to time, but so far the big Bastion raid is the biggest incident we've had.

Tenalach teaches permaculture as well as some spiritual classes and teachings on the weekend. I can see now why she was well-known back in Southern Illinois. I didn't realize it at first because she's not pretentious in the slightest. But she always has these interesting and unexpected insights, whether she's talking about composting human wastes or reflecting on the deeper meaning of life. She's very engaging. Honestly, I would go study with her if I weren't so busy with everything else.

All of our most basic green features here at Synergy Central are complete, or about as complete as they can be until we get more gardening supplies and our plants and fungi have more time to grow. About half of the building is still kept as residential space, most of it currently unused. A few of the original tenants left, and the rest joined the Synergists, so now we don't have to differentiate between tenants and Synergists anymore. The rest of the building has been converted into indoor greenhouse space, work space, meeting space, and space for the composting toilets, kitchen scrap composting, rainwater storage, and so on. The upper roof is almost entirely filled with solar modules. The lower roof has a few solar module pavilions as well as a lot of garden space. The old pool has been turned into a small aquaculture project with fish and plants in it. It seems a bit strange to me, but I like the idea from a practical perspective, and it seems to be working.

Really, all things considered, everything seems to be going well. We are recovering nicely from the Bastion raid and making progress on several of our projects. Most of what's left here at Synergy Central is just expanding what's already here, so some of the emphasis has shifted to helping Havana and Roads, who are still getting set up. A part of me wants to just take it all at face value and assume that everything is okay.

But there's something in the air – a certain tension, like we're all waiting for the other shoe to drop. Here in Miami, Bastion attacked us recently, and we assume they were told to by the government, so maybe they'll try again. Thousands of people were arrested in the nationwide Purge, and there were some deaths too, so there's this heavy sense across the country that no one who takes action on global warming is really safe anymore. There are a lot of people in the streets, but it's more subdued now, and they've had to find smaller, more scattered areas where they won't be teargassed, peppersprayed, beaten, etc. Nobody knows exactly what the next move is, but everybody can tell that this conflict isn't over. It's just getting started, and it's only a matter of time before it gets crazy again.

If this is the calm before the storm, I'll take it. A few good days of what passes for normal in this city can go a long way. Here's hoping we get a lot of good work done while the weather is calm.

INDEFINITE DETENTION
October 17, 2030 at 22:16

We received some disturbing news today. All of the thousands of people who were arrested in the "Green Purge" earlier this week are being detained indefinitely as domestic terrorists.

The news reached Synergy Central a couple of hours before it became public knowledge. Several lawyers in Miami Diaspora have been working with a few other lawyers from around the country to form a legal defense team for the people arrested in these raids. The legal team has been trying for days to get more detailed information about who was in custody where and how to contact them. They were starting to assume that it was indefinite detention, but they heard official news early this morning. It took them a couple of hours to confirm the news and release a public statement, but we found out almost immediately through our contacts in Miami Diaspora.

So what does this mean?

The legal team was outraged. Everybody I know is outraged. Not surprised, of course. This isn't the first time an American citizen has been subjected to indefinite detention as a terrorism suspect. But it's usually just one or two. This is the first time so many people have been detained for such frivolous reasons. Keep in mind that as far as we can tell, some of these people have never even been involved in any type of direct action or civil disobedience. Sure, some were involved in demonstrations, but others were just "advocating" or "assisting" in some way.

Basically, if you advocate finally ending our use of fossil fuels, you might disappear.

¡Dios mío! What is this country coming to? I love this country, but things like this make me scared to even live here anymore.

One of the scariest things to me is that we probably won't know anytime soon who has been detained. If someone has green leanings, and they disappeared this week, then they were probably arrested. But can we be sure? Maybe they fled and they're out there somewhere, going underground, freezing to death in an alley, out in the woods somewhere, who knows. Or maybe they were wounded in a raid and they're in a hospital or morgue somewhere. If they weren't carrying their ID — because they got woken up in the middle of the night by police or Bastion! — it might take a while to figure out who they are and what happened to them.

The lawyers are insisting that the government release the names of everyone who they arrested or attempted to arrest. But that involves paperwork, of course, and paperwork takes time. In the meantime, they're confident that almost two thousand people have been affected, but possibly twice that number. They just set up a public website and phone number to help people who think someone they know has been arrested. The reports are trickling in.

It will take time to sort this all out. I half-expected another surge of wild demonstrations in response to this. But actually the demonstrations have started to quiet down. Everybody here at Synergy Central is pretty tense. I've heard it's the same in other cities. People are upset by this revelation, and they want to do something, but they also don't want to get disappeared. There have been a few outbursts of spontaneous protest and even violence from the people whose friends and families are being indefinitely detained. But most people are just taking a deep breath, sorting it all out, and figuring out their next move.

I know that's what I'm doing. I'm really wondering what to do next. I have no idea. What do you do when your government starts getting more and more aggressive with its use of things like no-knock raids, indefinite detention, treating green-minded people as terrorists, and so on?

Right now, all I know how to do is demand for those people to be set free and keep working on my positive projects in the meantime. But really, we can't keep going on like this. Something needs to change.

LOSSES
October 20, 2030 at 23:42

I have a heavy heart today. My heart has often been heavy since Hurricane Florence changed so many lives. But today, my heart is heavier than usual.

Bastion attacked again this morning.

We knew this would happen sooner or later. At this point, we're the most prominent green group in Miami. They already hit us once. We assumed they would try again eventually. But of course, we didn't know the details.

We expected a night raid. That seems to be what they do in most places — strike hard and fast under the cover of darkness. We also expected an attack on either Synergy Havana or Synergy Roads because they're both lower to the ground and not as well-defended.

That's not what happened.

We didn't know this at first, but today was the start of another round of arrests. It was the second phase of the Green Purge, or "Operation Decisive Sweep" as it's officially known. Several dozen locations across the country were hit, including some of the public Occupy-style encampments where people have been discussing what to do about the climate crisis — and now the detention crisis.

The local Bastion troops started by attacking our speedboat, the Clover, with overwhelming force. Jess and a few other people were traveling between Synergy Central and Synergy Havana when out of nowhere, a few dozen people in tactical gear appeared out of nowhere and started assaulting them from surrounding buildings with teargas and rubber bullets. They put on their gas masks and tried to fight back, but there was no hope. Everyone survived, thank God, but they were all injured in the fight and quickly captured. One of the witnesses recognized Jess and told me she was taken into custody alive and mostly okay, although she was clutching her arm in pain as they dragged her away.

As soon as they captured our crew on the Clover, they sped away in a few small, fast speedboats to join in the attack on Synergy Central.

The attack on Clover happened so quickly that they weren't able to tell us what was happening. But we've been keeping in constant audio contact with everyone who's out in the field, so we heard some commotion and knew something was up. Before the attack over there had even finished though, Bastion started hitting Synergy Central.

True to my word, I sent out a distress signal citywide the moment I knew we were under attack. It turns out that may have saved all of our lives.

From what we can tell, Bastion had two plans. Plan A was to take Synergy Central with overwhelming force. We've been watching their patrols, so we have some sense of how many troops they have and where they are. But they must have snuck people around in plain clothes or underground tunnels or something. Because they had about twice as many people as we expected in the office building across the street. It was at least four dozen people, maybe more. They all attacked at once, and more people quickly joined them from other parts of Brickell.

They knew better than to go wading in through the front door for another taste of the Zapper. So instead, they started by firing a few live grenades at us from across the street.

I don't know if you've ever heard live grenades before. Given the way things are going in this country, maybe you have. I had never heard them before and they seemed even louder than the concussion grenades. I was near the top of the building when they hit and it still sounded loud to me. I felt the explosions.

Luckily, we had planned for this. A casual observer would see all the lights and activity on the lower floors of the building and assume that we were all concentrated down there. But actually, this was mostly an illusion. We do have some work spaces and offices down there, but especially after the Bastion raid, we started moving everything to the upper floors. We kept some lights and some people down there, and we kept all the lights turned off all the time in our living quarters and offices upstairs. All of those late nights and early mornings in the dark upstairs paid off. Bastion focused their initial attack on the lower floors that were mostly not in use.

But no plan is perfect. We do keep guards in the lobby at all times, and people do sometimes use the lower floors as office and workshop space. During Bastion's initial assault, three people died and four were injured. The person I knew best was Murray, one of our original members from Southern Illinois. This was actually his first time at Synergy Central in a week or two and I was looking forward to seeing him for lunch. But then Bastion struck him down while he was doing nothing more threatening than teaching a few people about rainwater catchment systems.

After hitting the first few floors with a few live grenades, Bastion charged in, entering the building from the lobby and the neighboring office building, just like they did last time. Their explosions had successfully disabled the Zapper, but we had other plans in store for them.

The first few floors have a few sturdy metal gates and barricades in the hallways and stairwells. This slows down travel on these floors even when you have the keys. When you don't have the keys, it really slows you down. While Bastion was breaking down the gates with power tools, we were scrambling to our defensive positions.

It's a good thing, too, because we didn't realize that we were about to be hit from above too.

Planes and helicopters have been scarce in Miami since Hurricane Florence. We talked about the possibility of Bastion attacking us by helicopter, but we didn't take it too seriously. We just kept a few doors locked just in case. While we were scrambling downstairs to fight off the ground troops, about a dozen of them were entering from the upper roof of the building, deposited there by a helicopter.

It was chaos. When we heard the commotion of the helicopter and explosions upstairs, we knew we were trapped between two teams, one above and one below. There were a few dozen of us in the building at the time, and we had to make a quick decision about what to do. The Synergists is mostly a horizontally organized group with everyone making decisions cooperatively. But we do have some structure for moments like this. Harold is usually in charge of defense, but he was off at Synergy Havana with Tenalach, so it was up to me.

I will always remember that moment. There I was, standing in a crowded hallway with a few dozen of my fellow Synergists. Some were armed, some weren't. Some had been in a fight before, some hadn't. All were caught up in a huge adrenaline rush. And they all looked to me for a decision about what to do.

¡Dios mío! I've started getting used to playing a leadership role around here. But I'm more of a civilian leader, not a Green Guard leader like Harold. I took a deep breath and did my best to stay calm while I wrapped my head around the situation. Then I told everybody to follow me down to the lower levels to fight off the team invading from below. And they did.

We had some defenses in place. The main defense was small holes cut in the floor to dump concussion grenades or other surprises on people on the lower floors. It's fairly easy to drop something down those holes, but a little harder for them to toss something up, though not impossible. We also had cameras in each hallway so we could see what was going on using our tablets. So we started dropping concussion grenades on them from above so that they would have to fall back.

This was obviously only a temporary solution. We didn't have very many of those grenades, just a couple on each floor. So then we had to toss Molotov cocktails down there too.

This was an insane idea, of course. We were setting fire to our own building. But we didn't have many options. Judging by the live grenades they used to make their entry into the building, we weren't even sure if they planned on capturing us or just killing us. I still wonder what they would have done if they'd made it up that far. But luckily, right around then, our luck changed.

They suddenly started retreating. Not just backing away from the holes where we were dumping unpleasant surprises on their heads. They actually started leaving the building. We watched in shock as the troops below us scurried back down the stairs and out of the building. Then we heard the helicopter come back to pick up the troops above us. If they'd kept at it for just a few more minutes, it would have ended in an ugly gun battle, probably with all of the Synergists dead or captured. Instead, the

Bastion troops all started retreating.

Why? They had to switch to Plan B.

Plan A was to take Synergy Central by force. But my distress signal apparently brought a lot of unwanted visitors to Brickell. Plan B was to hit us hard and fast, do some damage while they could, and then retreat to protect their clients in Brickell. As Bastion retreated, we heard automatic gunfire and explosions in the distance. I carefully peeked out a window to see what was happening.

When I looked down the street one way, I saw about fifty or sixty people from Synergy Havana coming our way. Some of them were wading and some were riding on various small boats and rafts. They were mostly unarmed, at least in terms of guns, but they were shouting and waving various improvised weapons at the retreating Bastion forces. There was actually a group of three of them who had crossbows, which I wasn't expecting. In the other direction, there were a few speedboats with armed men in suits zipping past the Bastion boats toward the heart of Brickell, exchanging gunfire with the Bastion troops as they gave chase.

I warned Bastion about this. I told them that if they attacked Synergy Central again, there would be consequences. And there were. The Synergists never initiate violence, but the same can't be said for the gangs. One or more of them decided to take advantage of the chaos for their own benefit. I don't know exactly what happened out there, but the banks and offices in downtown Brickell definitely got hit by a few bands of well-armed criminals while their defenses were weak. I've heard rumors that one of the buildings was robbed and some of the people inside taken hostage for ransom. That was never my intention, but that's what happens when Bastion goes around killing innocent gardeners and teachers and plumbers instead of protecting its clients from criminals.

I don't know how other people do this. How can anyone stand to watch their friends and neighbors get captured and killed like this? I can't stand it. After we put out the fires and made sure the building was safe, I saw what was left of my friend Murray's body. I could barely even recognize him. I never had a chance to say goodbye. And I don't know if I'll ever see mi querida Jess again. They have her. The people who blew up our lobby, trashed our biggest garden, and killed Murray. They took her. And they still have her.

My heart feels so heavy. And even though I know intellectually that it's all Bastion's fault, I still feel responsible. I don't know what I could have done differently. All I know is that I have to do something to set this right. We can't keep living under the threat of Bastion and Operation Decisive Sweep and everything else that's wrong with this city and this country. I said it before and I'll say it again. Something has to change. And we have to do whatever it takes to change it.

MARCH ON D.C.
October 22, 2030 at 23:54

I just watched the President's speech about Operation Decisive Sweep and our nation's response to global warming. I can't write for long, but I have to say a few things or I won't be able to sleep.

This is the first full speech that the President has given since the raids started. In each of our three Synergy Centers, we had a live showing of the speech. The one here at Synergy Central was indoors and mostly just consisted of fellow Synergists. There were a few dozen of us crowded into an expanded apartment that we've turned into a conference room. But the showings at Synergy Havana and Synergy Roads were public. They projected it onto big screens on the side of their buildings so that people from the neighborhoods could watch it. Most people still don't have power at home, so it was a big event. There were over a hundred people at Roads and several hundred at Havana. I've even heard that a Bastion team patrolling near Roads stopped nearby and watched from a distance. Everybody wanted to hear what he had to say.

It was mostly bad news. Honestly, I don't know how else to put it. Bad news.

One of the reasons I voted for him was because I thought he would actually do something serious about global warming. This was before Hurricane Florence, of course, so I wasn't as adamant about it yet. But I grew up in Miami while the ocean was slowly but surely reclaiming the city. I knew that we had to do something. It's now or never. And he gave such good speeches about how important it was to take action on global warming.

But now he says that we're not ready to quit fossil fuels. He says we need more time to transition to clean energy. He says that he sympathizes with "reasonable" people who advocate for clean energy, but that it's "unreasonable" to demand we stop using fossil fuels entirely within the next decade or two. He also says that as long as we're using fossil fuels as a major energy source, anyone who's engaging in direct action to shut down fossil fuel infrastructure is a threat to national security and must be treated as a terrorist.

He has such a way with words, doesn't he? My mother used to call it "pico de oro". Gift of the gab. Silver-tongued. He tells us that hundreds of thousands of Americans may need to be disappeared, but he makes it sound like he's on our side. He wants to help us, but his hands are tied.

So instead, he arrests us.

If you care so much about global warming, Mr. President, then why are your agents and officers coming for us instead of the fossil fuel tycoons?

I know it's not easy being in your shoes. There are people in this country who would try to impeach you if you sided with us against the fossil fuel industry. And who knows, they might succeed. But you're supposed to be a world leader. Follow the leadership of your people. Make the difficult choice. Work with us instead of against us.

But of course, the President has many advisors telling him to be "reasonable" too. And we all know who writes their paychecks.

Honestly, even the good news that he had to share was bad news in disguise. His so-called good news was that the government is going to release the names of the detained and make an effort to try each of them for specific crimes in a timely manner rather than just detaining them indefinitely. Some of them will surely be home in a couple of months, he says, and they're being kept in humane conditions until then. But he has not relinquished them to civilian courts and will not be doing so. They're being tried as terrorists. And any future Americans who engage in direct action against fossil fuel infrastructure will also be tried as terrorists. He even pointed out that people convicted of terrorism can't hold office, making a reference to the political candidates who have been arrested. Not good news.

And he didn't say this, but everybody knows that Congress and the Supreme Court are even more conservative than he is. They won't be challenging him on this anytime soon. Some will try, of course, but they will be outnumbered. For now. And some of the people who might have shifted that balance are currently detained, whereabouts unknown.

Before he even finished speaking, I knew that millions of my fellow Americans had to be thinking what I was thinking.

It's time for a march on D.C.

Sure enough, as soon as the speech ended, people started sending out all sorts of declarations and calls to action. Some of them must have been typing while they watched because they sent out these messages within moments of the end of the speech. The first call to action I read was sent by some members of Rising Tide who have evaded arrest so far. I keep seeing new statements each time I search. If you haven't had time to actually read any of the statements yet, the general idea is to reject the legitimacy of the President's approach and declare a march on Washington D.C. the weekend before the elections, which is coming up quickly.

It's going to be a crazy couple of weeks. I feel very torn about what to do personally. I can't imagine leaving Miami so soon after returning, especially when there's so much work to do here. But I'm sure at least some of the Synergists will go to D.C. to participate in this march.

It's a tough call, really. We need as many people as possible in D.C. to make this march count. If only a few thousand show up, they'll all get disappeared. We need to make this the largest march on D.C. in history. But we also need to keep as many people as possible in our local communities to make sure our various community projects don't get shut down or run out of steam while we're away. Doing both will take millions of very active and possibly high-risk participants. I bet everyone involved in any form of community organizing is making some tough decisions now. I'm no exception.

I need to get some sleep. It will still take me a while to fall asleep, but I'm tired, and I have to sleep so I'll be ready for the day tomorrow. Maybe I'll go out on the roof and sleep in what's left of our garden so I can see the stars and look out over the ocean. The ocean has always been a source of strength and comfort for me. And I could use it now more than ever. There are some rough waters ahead.

GOODBYE AGAIN, MIAMI
October 25, 2030 at 22:22

Everything's happening so fast. I don't have much time to write tonight because I have to be up before dawn tomorrow.

Why? Because I'm leaving Miami.

I've known for days that this was a possibility. Millions of people from across the country are mobilizing as we speak, slowly but surely making their way to Washington D.C., or at least the nearest state capital. People are packing into every type of vehicle imaginable — old and new, gas and electric, beat-up old sedan and sleek new sports car, second-hand station wagon and commercial bus. Some are even riding their bicycles or simply walking, going as far as they can get by next weekend.

The weekend before Election Day.

State and federal authorities are already starting to take measures to control traffic. They can't stop every single vehicle heading east, so they're doing some random stops and checkpoints along major routes looking for anything obvious — wanted fugitives, certain tools and supplies, anything indicating that you might be going to D.C. for the upcoming marches and demonstrations. They're not outlawing demonstrations entirely, but they're having one permitted march and rally that will be highly controlled and monitored. Anything else that happens that disrupts the flow of traffic or commerce in D.C. will be considered an act of terrorism. The President has gone on TV again calling for peaceful demonstrations and encouraging people to demonstrate in their own cities so as not to choke the nation's capital with millions of unruly guests.

But if millions of Americans are upset with the raids, the continued use of fossil fuels, the corruption in government, and so on, what better place to be than Washington D.C.? We are not the guests. It's our capital. The politicians are the guests. And most of them have overstayed their welcome.

For security reasons, I won't be disclosing any details about our travel plans until we get there. Honestly, I don't know the full details myself. My contacts in Miami Diaspora have connected me with a few people along the way who plan on helping everyone get to D.C. Since the authorities are starting to crack down on a few major interstate highways, this may involve taking the scenic route. But we'll get there.

So why did I decide to leave Miami? Sending a group of Synergists out to D.C. makes sense. Just about every community group of any type is sending some percentage of their members there. And random people who don't belong to any group are going too. But there are a few hundred Synergists now spread out between three centers. Why not send some of them instead? Why not stay here in the city that I love, the city I worked so hard to come back to, the city that I hope we can breathe new life into with our solar energy and urban gardens and other green projects?

I thought long and hard about this. Honestly, I almost didn't go. I spent about two hours last night talking it over with Ermete, who is always full of interesting ideas and one of the most genuinely kind human beings I've ever known. I've always felt a certain closeness to him, but ever since Jess was taken by Bastion, he's been my greatest source of inspiration and comfort. After talking to him for two hours up on the roof, alone together beneath a glowing blanket of stars, looking out together on the shimmering waters, I thought I would never leave this place again. I thought I would be happy to spend forever in this place. As crazy as it may seem, this sunken city is my home, my life, the place I want to be.

But then this morning, I saw two things that changed my mind.

The first was the children. Synergy Central is mostly filled with adults, but there were some children from Synergy Havana visiting today to see our solar system and what's left of our garden. I haven't had any children myself yet, but I find them interesting and endearing. They have such curious and playful minds — asking questions, exploring, climbing around on things and playing with random object until you tell them not to.

I was happy to see them. But then my heart sank when I overheard their teacher explaining why some of the garden had been damaged and what it meant for the community. She explained it in gentle terms, of course — words like "fighting" and "arresting" and "misunderstanding" rather than "attacking" and "disappearing" and "thought crimes". But explaining the damage lead to a simple lesson about the violence we face simply for trying to create a world that doesn't run on fossil fuels and factory farms and God knows what else. It seemed so matter of fact, like learning about the sun and the wind and the rain. This is just what happens sometimes. Sometimes they come and arrest people we know, and damage our houses and gardens, and we may feel scared, and we may go hungry for a little while, but we carry on as best as we can. It was a very important lesson for the children given recent events. But somehow I couldn't stand it. I actually walked away with tightness in my chest and tears in my eyes for the first time since they took Jess. I didn't mean to disrupt her lesson, so I hope nobody noticed. But something about it really hit me.

And then the last straw was Bastion.

After seeing the children, I went back to my office and looked out my window, lost in thought. After calming down for a few minutes, I noticed several big Bastion boats docked in front of a nearby building. They weren't engaging in their usual patrolling. The troops were going in and out of the building, loading up a bunch of supplies. They only left behind a few people while several dozen of them piled into the boats with their assault rifles in hand and pulled away. It took a few moments for me to realize what I was actually seeing.

They were leaving.

Not all of them, of course. We showed them what happens when you leave Brickell undefended for even a few minutes. But I made a few phone calls and confirmed that Bastion was sending a large contingent north, either to Tallahassee or maybe even to D.C. They knew that something big was coming and they were being mobilized to stop it.

If I thought like a normal person — a person with some sense of survival — I would have taken that as a sign to stay. Instead, I had the exact opposite response. As I saw those boats speed away, I felt a sinking feeling that only deepened when I made my phone calls to confirm what I already knew.

I have to go.

The fact that they're pulling some Bastion troops from Miami tells me two things. Number one, they are so afraid of this mass march that they're leaving an entire major city vulnerable to rebels and looters. And

I bet we're not the only ones. Number two, if they're sending more people, we need to send more people. This may be one of the most important marches in the history of this country. It may decide the course of this coming election, the course of our nation's action on global warming, and so many other related things. Whatever happens will lead to either a giant leap back or a giant leap forward. We can't let Bastion run the show. We have to be there in overwhelming numbers, and we have to make our voices heard.

So I decided to go. And then I decided to spend the rest of the day looking for extra volunteers throughout the city. We're already sending all of the Synergists we can spare, but now we're finding more people who want to go to D.C. and need help getting there. Our resources are very limited, but we're doing what we can. I just hope it will be enough.

If anything happens to me on the way there, this may be my last entry. Thank you to everyone who has read this blog. Writing these entries and talking to the people who read them has been a major inspiration for me. Thank you for all of your support. Thank you for all that you do in your own cities. Whatever happens in D.C., I hope you'll all keep creating communities where people work with each other and with the sun, wind, and water to build a good life together. Here's to the day when we all live that way.

ANTICIPATION
October 21, 2030 at 23:42

We made it safely to Washington D.C.

It was quite a trip. The Liminals let us use the old electric bus and van that the original Synergists rode into Miami. Synergy Roads also supplied us with two more electric vans for some of the new volunteers who are joining us for the march.

We had to avoid a few major cities, both because of the traffic and because of the random stops and checkpoints along the way. It took a long time, but there were some beautiful spots in rural Georgia and the Carolinas. When we reached southern Virginia, we passed on the bus and van on to a local community center in exchange for a few smaller vehicles that would draw less attention.

The security approaching D.C. was outrageous. It was obvious that there was a state of emergency. Inbound traffic on the interstates was almost at a standstill due to the checkpoints, armored personnel carriers, and sheer number of vehicles. None of our people got arrested, but it put us on edge.

In order to find places to stay close to the city, we had to split up. I'm here with Bridget, one of the original Synergists, and a few newer recruits who I don't know as well but have gotten to know better on the trip over here. We're going to be sleeping on the floor of a small church with what looks like about a hundred other people. It'll he cozy, but we're all here for similar reasons, so it works. There's this energy among the people that's hard to describe — a tangible sense of anticipation. You can hear it in people's voices, see it in their eyes, feel it in their body language. Some are talking about politics. Some are talking about the weather. Some are talking about anything but the march. But no matter what they're talking about, its obvious how wired they all are, each with their own person mix of excitement, fear, anger, hope, and most of all, longing for change.

I feel it too.

So now, we wait. Tomorrow is the big day. Nobody knows for sure how many people are marching, but most of the people outside of Fox News are saying this will be by far the biggest march in the history of the country. I guess we'll see. Whatever happens, it's good to know we're not alone. Wish us luck.

The Struggle For The Capitol
November 2, 2030 at 18:43

I'm alive and free and mostly okay. Phone and internet is down everywhere, so I'm not sure if or when I can post this message. But I want to write it before my battery dies.

The city of Washington D.C. is under siege. That may seem like a colorful metaphor, but honestly, it's a fairly accurate description. Before communications went down, we heard multiple sources estimate that between three and four million people participated in the march on D.C. That's at least double the previous record. Ordinary life in Washington D.C. has shut down while a few million guests make their presence known in our nation's capital.

It all started yesterday, the Friday before the election. After a few hours of sleep on the floor of a church sanctuary, we all headed into the city. Our team from Miami split up into two groups: a group of twenty-one of us who are Synergists and a group of twelve volunteers from around Miami who didn't have any other way to get here. We traveled all the way into the city together, but we decided to split up when we reached the march.

The march itself was amazing. In the hopes of placating all of these "unruly guests", the government approved a permit for a single official march through the heart of the city. It started at noon and had a very long route in order to accommodate as many people as possible. The route was lined by a mix of police, military, Bastion, and probably other security personnel. So many of them were wearing similar black tactical gear that they tended to look alike at a certain point. An occupying army. There were physical barricades along the edges of the route protected by police vehicles and armored personnel carriers. There was also a massive swarm of helicopters and various types of drones buzzing overhead. They created a constant buzz that fluctuated in intensity but never quite went away. I've heard that all air traffic was restricted to military and Bastion only, but of course some media outlets and individuals snuck in a few surveillance drones too. I doubt that anyone was foolish enough to sneak a passenger aircraft into such a tense situation. I have no doubt that they would have been shot down.

It's hard to describe what the mood was like on the streets. Everyone I saw was riled up — shouting, chanting, singing, dancing, even climbing on street lights and walls to get better pictures or unfurl banners. The chants, signs, and so on talked about everything related to the broad struggle for climate justice: "Free The Disappeared"; "Free The Candidates"; "End Extractivism"; "Stop Global Warming"; "Fossil Fuels Have Got To Go"; "Sun, Wind, Water"; "Remember Florence"; "Remember Michael"; "Save Bangladesh"; "Save The Coasts"; "Here Comes The Tide"; and more. There were people with giant puppets and people in colorful costumes like the Lorax, polar bears, butterflies, green superheroes, and who knows what else. It was amazing.

To a casual observer, it might have seemed like the world's biggest party. But even during the peaceful times at the beginning and middle of the march, you could feel this biting tension in the air. There was a desperation haunting the faces of all but the most boisterous of marchers. We were marching under the watchful eye of tens of thousands of heavily armed and armored security personnel. On that first day, there seemed to be at least three different layers of them: the large number of police drawn in from several surrounding states who were coordinating the front lines of crowd control; the Bastion troops just behind them, ready to step in with heavier gear and harsher tactics if necessary; and the D.C. National Guard clustered around major landmarks, ready to use lethal force as necessary to protect key buildings and maintain continuity of government. And then there were the drones — planes and copters, armed an unarmed, seen and unseen. The drones were a constant reminder that we were seen by our government not as demonstrators, but as insurgents. The same machines that have been putting down insurgencies overseas for my entire life were now putting them down at home. Openly declaring our green slogans and demands for change in this atmosphere of surveillance and military readiness felt equal parts defiant and terrifying.

Given this atmosphere of tension, it's amazing that things went as well as they did for most of the march. But then at the end of the march, we were attacked.

The first attack came from the Constitutional Militia Coalition. This national militia started as a bunch of regional coalitions like the one I had some encounters with during my time in Southern Illinois. Over the past few months, the rapid increase in green activism has driven their leadership into an anti-green frenzy, leading them to set aside some of their other differences and unite in their opposition to the Green Front. Everything up until now has been mostly law-abiding, so we thought they would just be thankful that the government was cracking down on us. But that wasn't good enough for them. We had to be eliminated. So they decided to attack the march.

The casualties were severe. I have no idea how many CMC attacked us, or how many of our people died, because we lost all communication shortly after the attack. According to the estimates I've heard by word of mouth, there must have been a few hundred CMC holed up in various buildings along the parade route. Some people are saying that the government must have been involved, but it really didn't seem like they knew what was happening. There were just suddenly live grenades and improvised explosives and bursts of gunfire all around us. I saw explosions about fifty yards in front of me and heard more behind me. Hundreds of people were killed or seriously wounded just within the parts that I could see. It was like a scene out of a war movie. I have never been so scared in my entire life. There was just suddenly fire and smoke and flying debris and bloody bodies everywhere. It felt like there was nowhere safe to go. Luckily, none of the Synergists were killed, but five of us were wounded, and I think we all had the same terrible ringing in our ears. We had spread out a little bit in case something like this happened, so some of us got it worse than others. But those were some deafening explosions that affected us all. It was more damage than anyone other than CMC could have expected.

At that point, all hell broke loose. The marchers were trapped between the explosions and the barricades along the edges of the route. Police and some of the marchers started opening fire on the CMC snipers hidden inside the buildings. It was pure chaos for about a minute or two as most people just tried to get the hell out of the way of the violence. Bastion troops didn't seem to care about the snipers, instead using flashbang grenades and rubber bullets to keep the fleeing marchers from overwhelming the barricades. They were mostly successful, but I saw at least one place where the sheer number of people pushed over a barricade and overwhelmed the police and Bastion troops. The crowd didn't seem to be attacking the troops, just trampling them on their way out of the meat grinder. The troops who were still standing retreated into vehicles or buildings, trying in vain to stem the flow of humanity.

I tried to lead my fellow Synergists in the direction of the breach, but there's only so much leading you can do in a crazy situation like that. We were all barely able to keep track of one another while the crowd surged in the opposite direction, pushed away from the breach by Bastion firepower. Bridget and I had to drag Lou along with us because he'd been hit in the leg by some shrapnel and trampled by the panicked crowd. We ended up regrouping at a boarded-up storefront that was slightly set back from the crowd while we assessed the damage and figured out what to do.

We decided to split into two teams — one to seek shelter with the wounded and another to continue with the march. By that point, I was mostly fine, just a little bruised and shocked, so I decided to head up the forward group. Jalen came with me, as did six other people. Bridget headed up the retreating group and headed to a nearby church that we had heard was being used as a safe space during the march.

It took us a few minutes to figure out our next move. By the time we were split up, the situation had changed. I don't know what happened in other parts of the city, but we were a few blocks away from the Washington Monument, and we saw some police and Green Guard actually working together to shoot back at the CMC snipers. Everyone who wasn't armed was just trying to get as far away as possible, which was difficult because there were so many people and sounds of gunfire coming from several directions. The people on the ground with guns were getting into various small spots of cover behind bits of barricade and vehicles, occasionally firing up at some broken windows a few stories above street level.

Jalen called out to the Green Guard and they waved us over. We got as close as we could without being too exposed to the snipers across the street. Someone from the dozen or so Green Guard asked us to cover them while they sent a small team over to get inside the building.

Keep in mind here that I am by no means any type of soldier or police officer. Before we came to D.C. this weekend, I had only fired a gun about a dozen times as part of my crash course from Harold and others in basic weapons training. I'm more of a talker and organizer, not a fighter. But I did what I could. We all fired some shots at those broken windows at the same time while half a dozen people in Green Guard fatigues rushed across the street and broke through a door on the ground floor of the building. I don't know if they captured or killed the CMC snipers, but after a minute or two of gunfire inside the building, someone radioed down to their teammates that the situation was under control.

Jalen and I had a quick discussion with the other six Synergists who had come with us. We were all okay, more or less, so we decided to push ahead to the rallying point at the Lincoln Memorial.

While police and Green Guard were still dealing with pockets of CMC snipers lining the march route, many of the marchers made their way to the Lincoln Memorial. This is where we had originally planned to have a big rally with public speakers and so on. There was a tightly packed crowd of people spreading out as far as the eye could see. There was some more chaos as everyone figured out what to do in response to the attack on the march. About a half hour after the speeches were supposed to start, somebody finally came on to the big stage they'd prepared for the event and announced that about half of the people who were scheduled to speak were still missing. The front of the march had been attacked heavily, so there was some concern that some of the speakers may not have even survived. The ones who made it to the rallying point came on stage together to make a short but impassioned plea to the crowd, calling for everyone to gather their courage and remember why they came here. They demanded that all political prisoners be released immediately and all candidates have their names restored to the ballots for public office. After their statement, one of the organizers on the stage started announcing a few other updates about what had been going on in the city since the start of the march.

And then, the power went out.

When I say that the power went out, I mean the power really went out. As far as we can tell, it went out across the entire city. The speakers on the main stage started working on their backup power, but everyone else started talking among themselves about what to do next.

It reminded me of what I've heard about the Occupy general assemblies, but more chaotic and much, much bigger. Some of the crowd had scattered throughout D.C. as they fled the explosions and shootings, but there must have been a million or more people crowded around the Lincoln Memorial, the reflecting pool, the Washington Monument, all sorts of areas along the National Mall. We started talking in small groups ranging from a few dozen to a few hundred using the call and repeat style of grassroots communication. Honestly, there were often too many overlapping groups and messages for it to make any sense. It got confusing and jumbled at certain points. But we tried, and we eventually got some good conversations going. After a while, the groups all started talking to each other, mostly by shouting a short chant when a bunch of people came up with an idea that they thought was important. One group started leading all of the wounded to the Vietnam Veterans Memorial, which was becoming a gathering place for street medics and paramedics. Another group shouted that people who want to get in on a spontaneous massive direct action at the Capitol building should meet up at the World War II Memorial.

I don't know if it was just a coincidence or if they didn't like what we were saying. But this is about when the police and Bastion issued their first warning to disperse.

The warning came from many sources — a few armored vehicles on the streets, a few helicopters flying overhead, maybe even a few of the drones. Since it was being blasted from multiple sources at the same time, there was a surreal echoing. There were also suddenly some spotlights and flashing lights that were very disorienting.

The voice on the speakers told us that the permitted march and rally had drawn to a close. We were encouraged to disperse peacefully or we would be subject to arrest.

Nobody liked this idea, of course. At least nobody that I saw. Some people started leaving, but others shouted and screamed at them, pleading with them to stay and show their support. And together, as one big mass, the million or more of us who were left started marching toward the Capitol.

What happened next may have been even more chaotic than when CMC attacked, although there were far fewer deaths. We marched on the Capitol, surrounding the barricades on every side with a seemingly endless sea of humanity. The voices on the speakers warned us again that we had to disperse. As we shouted slogans at the mostly empty Capitol building, some people tried to push their way past the barricades. Police and Bastion troops responded forcefully with their shields and batons, trying to push the crowd back. But there were far too many of them, and they were far too determined. Some had gas masks, earplugs, and various objects that they were using as shields. They started climbing on the barricades and pushing their way through the mass of riot police on the front lines.

And then came the big attack.

I'd never seen or heard of anything like this at a demonstration. It would almost call it a less-lethal massacre, if there is such a thing. Helicopters and drones started swooping down from above, dropping an incredible amount of teargas, smoke bombs, and flashbangs throughout the entire crowd. There were also some armored vehicles using these obnoxious sound cannons that hurt my head and eventually made me vomit right there in the street as I tried to run away. One of the trucks started spraying massive amounts of this thick white foam that seemed to immobilize everyone it touched. Another one was chasing after people and pointing a big panel at them that was making them scream and cry and run away. I have no idea what exactly it was doing to them. I've heard it may have been microwaves or just a different type of sound cannon. Whatever it was, it was terrifying.

Everybody scattered. From what I saw and what I've heard since, they managed to clear just about everyone out of the area around the Capitol one way or another. Some of them were simply chased away, fleeing the area and maybe even leaving the city entirely. Others were taken away in big buses or just left there for hours on end in zip tie handcuffs or piles of white foamy goo.

So we scattered and retreated. Jalen and I managed to stick together, but we got separated from the other Synergists. We spent a few hours looking for them, but between the lack of internet and the heavy Bastion presence on the streets, we couldn't find them. We were both exhausted, so we spent the night hiding and recovering with about a dozen other survivors in a small infoshop not far from the National Mall. Power was still out for the entire city, and most places didn't have backup power, so we slept in the dark, on the floor, in a cluttered office surrounded by odd shapes and unfamiliar people. I had a headache, nausea, dehydration, a banged up knee, and probably some degree of shock, so I really needed the rest. As soon as I actually found a semi-comfortable position, I fell asleep and slept hard for about nine or ten hours, which is very unusual for me.

That was all yesterday. Not much has happened today. The power is still out everywhere and we're trying to figure out what to do next. I've been writing this entry off and on throughout the day as we rest and talk to our hosts. The people at this infoshop have been talking to other small groups with walkie talkies, short wave radio, and an app that communicates directly with other phones and devices in the area via wireless. They also sent out scouts a few times throughout the day to find out what's happening in the city. There is still a heavy presence of police, Bastion, and National Guard, but not as heavy as yesterday. Most of the demonstrators have gone into hiding. At this point, it sounds like people are torn between making another big push for the Capitol to make our demands or just fleeing the city and going home.

Honestly, it's a tough decision. Considering how easily they scattered us from the Capitol yesterday, I'm not sure there's much point in trying again. Then again, they may not be as ready for it this time. It's been almost a day, and they arrested thousands of people, including many people who they consider "organizers". So in their minds, this might all be over, or at least wrapping up. Maybe a sudden push would catch them off guard. Or maybe it will just get more of us hurt, arrested, or killed. With all that's happened, though, it just feels like this can't be how it ends. This can't end with thousands of small groups of people scattered throughout the city, hiding and licking their wounds, slowly but surely deciding to limp home. That feels wrong. But would it really accomplish anything if we took the Capitol? Or would it just get us all arrested or killed? Maybe it's better to go home while we still can and live to fight another day. That seems like the most likely outcome right now, but also the least satisfying. Is that really how the biggest march in our history — and maybe even the most important one — is going to end?

I guess we'll see.

NOVEMBER 3
November 3, 2030 at 23:42

The Third of November may someday be recognized as one of the most important days in our history, right up there with the Fourth of July. Maybe that's just the endorphins talking, but I don't know how history can view it any other way.

Two days ago, three million people marched through Washington D.C. calling for climate justice. We were violently attacked by anti-green militias. We were harassed and dispersed by government and corporate security forces. The arrests and intimidation reduced our numbers to about a million. We were driven from the Capitol and scattered throughout the city. We spent a day regrouping and discussing our next move. Then, at the break of dawn on the Third of November, we made our next move.

We decided to occupy the Capitol.

Some refused to participate in the action. Since Congress wasn't currently in session, and all of our legislators had surely fled to various bunkers and safe houses around the country, this would be a largely symbolic act. Even if we did somehow manage to occupy the building, we wouldn't magically gain control over the government.

But maybe there was a little magic afoot, because that's not too far from what happened.

I'm sure a million different people will tell this story a million different ways. I don't have a complete picture of what happened because communications were down. I'm only just now learning some of the bigger details from people who did have better access to TV and the internet, which obviously can only be trusted so far. But here's my take on today's events.

After the march was attacked and dispersed, the demonstrators who stayed in the city were communicating with each other in various ways: walkie talkies, short wave radios, apps that communicate with each other wirelessly even when there's no phone or internet service. The government or Bastion made some effort to block these communications, but they weren't entirely successful. I also have no doubt that they were listening. But we talked anyway.

Honestly, the fact that government and corporate agents were listening may have worked in our favor. After the first attempt to take the Capitol, most of us were feeling deeply discouraged, myself included. It seemed like everyone was about ready to pack up and go home. Maybe that lead the security forces to switch from crowd control mode to mop-up mode. Or maybe not. Who knows.

What I do know is that in the wee hours of the night, while many of us were sleeping, support grew for the idea of one more attempt at taking the Capitol. By the time I woke up, it was still only an idea, a suggestion, a bit of wishful thinking. Less than an hour later, we had the Capitol surrounded again.

The sound of helicopters and drones had almost fallen silent during the night. But as we gathered at the Capitol, all of those government and corporate aircraft returned, filling the sky with an incessant buzzing that set everyone on edge. There were visibly fewer black-clad troops guarding the barricades this morning, but it was still an intimidating sight — a wall of thousands of heavily armed troops backed up by armored vehicles, various aircraft, and the advanced crowd control technology that had dispersed us so thoroughly before.

At first, I didn't even realize that Bastion had entirely taken over the front line duties. The actual police were nowhere to be seen. After it all went down, I heard rumors that the police went on a limited strike, agreeing to fight the remaining CMC in the city but refusing to deal with the crowd anymore. I don't know if this is true or not, but the rumor is that fighting side by side with the Green Guard to save their own lives helped sway the police in favor of the demonstrators. Most of them probably had some sympathy for us anyway. They just needed an excuse to justify siding with a bunch of "unruly guests" who seemed to be breaking the law. And at the end of the day, these people signed up to be police officers, not soldiers in a war zone. Being thrust into a wildly dangerous firefight between green and anti-green militias may have been enough to make them go on strike regardless of which side they supported.

Anyway, maybe we'll find out more details in the coming days as Congress conducts its hearings. For whatever reasons, the police weren't there this morning. It was thousands of Bastion troops backed up by thousands of National Guard.

There wasn't much hesitation on the part of the demonstrators. Jalen and I were hiding out nearby, so we got there while the crowd was still gathering. As soon as the crowd swelled to stretch as far as the eye could see, people near the front started shouting "Here Comes The Tide! Here Comes The Tide!" and surging forward into the "no protest" area in front of the barricades.

There also wasn't any hesitation on the part of the Bastion troops. The ones in the front raised their riot shields while the ones behind them opened fire with a variety of munitions: rubber bullets, electroshock bullets, bean bags, and even some weird ones like little rings filled with gas. They also had a few new handheld weapons that used microwaves, or pulsed energy, or who knows what else. In the back of my mind, as we all charged forward, I felt like we were all guinea pigs in some Bastion experiment. Which "non-lethal" weapons work best at controlling a crowd of a million people in an urban environment? I'm sure some unscrupulous lab geeks were watching live video feeds and taking copious notes.

As for me, I was hit twice by rubber bullets, at least twice that I remember. Don't let anyone tell you that those bullets are harmless toys. One hit me square in the chest, which knocked the wind out of me and bruised my breast severely. I was left gasping for breath for a while as other people rushed past me. The other rubber bullet grazed my head, which hurt like hell and left me dazed for a moment as I figured out what the hell had just happened. If I'd been standing about an inch to the left, it could have shattered my temple or hit me in the eye! What's wrong with these people?

They kept knocking us down, but we kept coming. There were just too many of us. Some people had improvised shields that they started bashing against the Bastion shield wall, trying to push their way through the barricades. Just like on Friday, various aircraft started closing in and dropping additional teargas, smoke bombs, and flashbangs on the crowd below.

But then our first miracle of the day happened.

Suddenly, the sky was full of these strange green aircraft. Each one was about the size of a watermelon, but they were all shaped like some type of fat metal insects, with multiple arms that flailed in the wind and flashed bright lights up at the sky. Hundreds of them started pouring out of nearby buildings. A few of them were set loose from the crowd itself. Rumor has it that an international team of tech geeks came up with the idea weeks ago and worked with a few small teams on the ground in

D.C. to pull it off. I'd bet any money that Ermete was involved, but he never even told me about the project. Sneaky.

These green bugs swarmed around all of the other flying craft, ganging up on a few at a time until the targets pulled away or crashed into buildings. It was actually dangerous to the crowd at times as the target drones smashed into buildings and tumbled into the crowd below. Some of our people probably got hurt in the process. But honestly, I doubt it was very many people. Most of the green bugs survived for long enough to move on to the helicopters. The helicopters, of course, had little patience for the swarms. They opened fire, shooting down some of the green bugs as they approached. But ultimately, most of the green bugs got through. The helicopters retreated, if only to regroup and try again.

For about a minute, most of the people I saw on the ground took a break from their fighting to look up at this aerial battle. Once it was clear that the green swarm was winning, at least for the time being, the crowd went wild. I did too. I was yelling, cheering, even jumping up and down in excitement at the sight of it. But then I realized that little creatures may have created a narrow window of opportunity. So I turned back to the Capitol. Jalen wasn't far from me, so I motioned for him to follow me and we continued the push forward.

I can only imagine how the Bastion troops felt at that moment. They seemed so intimidating and invincible to us at the time, but we outnumbered them at least a hundred to one. They must have felt threatened by the loss of air support, so some people in the back stepped forward and started firing lethal rounds into the crowd.

It was another senseless loss of life. At this point, I was still over a block away from the front lines, so I didn't really see the worst of it. But it must have been ugly. I heard the shots and eventually saw some of the bodies. Bastion just opened fire on the crowd with lethal rounds, killing dozens of people and wounding hundreds more in a very short amount of time. Assault rifles are ruthlessly efficient machines, after all. They weren't firing indiscriminately, either. I could see some Bastion troops from their positions on top of armored vehicles. They were clearly taking the time to aim, presumably shooting the closest demonstrators one by one until they went down. Some people near the front of the crowd also pulled out small weapons and started firing back, but they were clearly at a disadvantage. It was the start of what would have been a tremendous bloodbath.

That's when the second miracle of the day happened.

I had all but forgotten about the National Guard troops. They were far behind the barricades, positioned tightly around the Capitol building itself, standing at the ready in case the Bastion front lines fell. But when Bastion started firing lethal rounds, the National Guard stepped into action. I don't know if Bastion had broken the rules of engagement laid out by the government, or if the National Guard commanders got tired of watching Americans gunned down in the streets by mercenaries, or some combination of the two. But the shift was very sudden. I could see some of the National Guard troops in the distance on the steps of the Capitol. They all raised their weapons at the Bastion lines while some officer barked orders through a bullhorn. After a few moments of back and forth between Bastion and the National Guard, the Bastion troops gradually stopped firing. There was about a minute of tense silence before a voice boomed out of a few dozen of the armored vehicles nearby.

"The National Guard has informed us that our security services are no longer needed at this time. We do, however, retain our God-given right to self-defense. Please allow Bastion personnel and property to leave the area in a safe and orderly manner. Any acts of aggression will be responded to in kind. Thank you for choosing Bastion as your security solution."

For a moment, there was a stunned silence. When the Bastion troops actually started stepping back from the barricades and getting down from their perches on top of armored vehicles, the crowd all around me started cheering and shouting in joy. People near the front — including me — started rushing to tend to the wounded. But the people farther back who had a lot less wounded to deal with started singing and chanting.

There was a period of maybe fifteen or twenty minutes where people on all sides just stopped and recovered for a while. Jalen had a serious bullet wound to his good arm, so I spent some time using his med kit to clean and bandage the wound for him. I'm not very experienced with first aid, but I have basic training, and he was still conscious and alert enough to give me guidance and support. He also pointed out that I had a fairly serious gash on my thigh, which honestly I don't remember getting. I cleaned and bandaged that too.

While Bastion troops started loading into vehicles and marching away in columns, a few of the National Guard troops started setting up these big white walls at major intersections near the Capitol. At first I thought it might be some new type of barricade, but it was very flimsy and didn't even begin to cover the intersections. But then I realized that they were big video screens. Some of the government's sonic trucks started rolling up next to these screens to provide the audio for what came next. A few of the helicopters came back to provide audio for the people blocks and blocks away from us who couldn't see any screens or hear the audio up front.

And that's when the third and final miracle happened.

After a few minutes, two faces appeared on the screen. One was the Speaker of the House. The other was the Green Party candidate for President – who I should mention no one had seen or heard from since the start of the Purge! After both women introduced themselves, the Speaker of the House spoke.

"My fellow Americans, I come bearing good news. Your actions have moved many hearts and minds in this great nation, including the hearts and minds of many of my colleagues in the House and Senate. While we may disagree with your methods, we have come to understand and share some of your grievances. Therefore, I am pleased to announce that I have personally negotiated the immediate release of the majority of individuals arrested during Operation Decisive Sweep."

Everyone started shouting and cheering. Some wounded people who should have stayed immobile started limping and hopping around in their excitement. For a moment, all I could think about was Jess. I had to struggle to pay attention and strain my ears just to hear the rest of the announcement, which was soon posted online.

"A few of the people being released today are still facing serious charges. These charges will be resolved in civilian courts. Unfortunately, I've also prepared articles of impeachment against the President of the United States. I say unfortunately because this is a sad day for this great nation. We've had a hard time finding bipartisan support for anything in Congress lately, but there is growing bipartisan support for the idea that three million Americans shouldn't be declared enemy combatants. We will release the prisoners, most of whom have been wrongly arrested. And we'll work much harder now to resolve your concerns about the climate. Sooner or later, this great nation of ours must switch to 100% clean, green energy. It's time to admit that the era of fossil fuels is drawing to a close. The sacrifices you've made to remind us of the urgency of this transition are greatly appreciated."

Later in the day, a lot of pesky details would occur to me. How soon is "sooner or later"? Why did a few prisoners stay in indefinite detention? Why did some of the ones released still have charges pending against them? But in that moment, hearing those words felt wonderful. It felt like victory.

We actually did end up occupying the Capitol for the rest of the day. There were some police and National Guard in and around the building in case anything went wrong, and there were certain parts of the building we didn't have access to. But hundreds of people at a time filtered through the building, including the House and Senate chambers. The backup generators had the whole place lit up like it was any other day of the year. After spending a while without power, it was a bit surreal. Some people just treated it like a regular tour, but others took it more seriously, organizing as many people as possible into big public assemblies to discuss our next steps in search of climate justice. I participated in that for a while, but I couldn't resist taking a break for a couple of minutes to see what it was like to stand behind the big podium in the House chamber. It was one of my favorite memories of the day, standing up there and looking out at my fellow green demonstrators as they discussed public policy right there in the heart of the Capitol. It was beautiful.

At the end of the day, though, it was time to regroup and start making our way home.

Power was still out in most of the city, but phone service was back online. Jalen and I spent a few hours tracking down our fellow Synergists. We did manage to account for all of them eventually, but some of it was bad news. Two were dead. Four others were too badly wounded for a trip out of town. I made a few calls to my friends in Miami Diaspora and was able to find someone in D.C. to help take care of the wounded, although it may take us a while to figure out how to get them back to Miami. In the meantime, those of us who are still mobile decided to head home as soon as possible.

There's still so much work to do. In a way, this feels like an ending. We mobilized a record number of people in the pursuit of climate justice. It sounds like it may even encouraged a significant shift in our economic and political systems. But on another level, now that the endorphins are wearing off and I'm resting comfortably on the ride home, I have some time and energy for reflection. And the more I think about it, the more I realize that this isn't an ending. It's actually a beginning.

So many things are possible now. We've demonstrated widespread support for climate action. We've pushed hard against the many people in government and industry who have been slowing down and stopping action on climate change. We've even created some serious short-term changes. But really, all that we've done is create an opening for the real work to start.

It's time to once and for all end our reliance on fossil fuels. It's time to power our infrastructure with solar, wind, and water. It's time to shift from industrial agriculture and factory farming to more clean and humane ways of feeding and clothing ourselves. It's time to create the cooperative and community-based economic and political systems that we need to create social justice, environmental justice, and climate justice. The transition will take a tremendous amount of hard work — but it's good, honest work. That's more than anyone can say for the industries that profit by harming the health of workers, communities, the climate, and the diverse ecosystems that support all life on this planet.

It's time to start the real work: the work of resilience and resistance. Are you ready?

I've had a rough week. Honestly, I've had a rough couple of months. But I'm very ready to start this work. I also feel very fortunate to have a place to go to where I can work on all of these projects and then some. It's very helpful to have an all-purpose community center where people can learn about, talk about, and act on all of these ideas. We've made some serious progress at creating three such centers in Miami. If there's a place like Synergy Central near you, let today be the day that you get involved there. If you don't, send me an email sometime and I'll see what I can do to help you start one. It's not easy, but it's well worth it. You'll meet a lot of interesting people and make some amazing friends along the way.

Now that I've written all of this down, I'm going to take a break from writing for a while. If you're one of my long-time readers, thank you so much for your support. It has helped make everything else I do possible. Feel free to come down to Miami sometime and stop by Synergy Central to see what we're up to. In the meantime, I wish you the best of luck in your journey.

ABOUT THE AUTHOR

My name is Treesong. I'm a father, author, talk radio host, and Real Life Superhero. I live in Carbondale, Southern Illinois. I write novels, short stories, and poetry, mostly about the climate.

Learn more about my other books, poetry, and Real Life Superhero adventures by connecting with me online at treesong.org.

OTHER BOOKS BY TREESONG

CHANGE

What does global warming look like in a world full of magic, superheroes, and secret societies?

Sarah Athraigh, an environmental activist from Southern Illinois, stumbles into the midst of a hidden war between occult factions that are grappling with the root causes and dire consequences of climate change. As she goes on the run, she soon finds herself on a journey of discovery, searching for the unusual allies and innovative ideas that will help her to make a difference for the better in a dangerous world.

Change is a contemporary fantasy tale featuring a strong female lead, real life superheroes, secret societies, modern magic, political protests, the power of music, and a colorful cast of characters that Sarah meets along the way as she searches for solutions to the climate crisis.

CLI-FI PLUS

Cli-Fi Plus is a climate fiction anthology with an emphasis on genre and theme crossovers. Each short story combines elements of cli-fi with elements of more established genres and themes in sci-fi and literary fiction. The result is an entertaining read that keeps you on the edge of your seat and leaves you wondering what will come next in the real-life climate crisis.

What does a cli-fi alien story look like? What does a cli-fi robot story look like? What does a cli-fi zombie story look like? What does a cli-fi time travel story look like? What does a cli-fi political thriller look like? What does literary cli-fi look like? Find the answers to these questions and more in Cli-Fi Plus!

READ MORE OF TREESONG'S FICTION AND POETRY
AND LEARN MORE ABOUT HIS SUPERHERO ADVANTURES
AT TREESONG.ORG